Main Menu

Start Reading

Table of Contents

Acknowledgments

Copyright Information

Contact Information

Chapter 1 - Aja

Growing up wasn't easy for me at all. I feel sorry for any child who has to grow up with a crackhead for a mother.

My name is Aja Jackson, and life has dealt my brother and me, a shitty hand courtesy of our mother. Gail Jackson is a sorry ass excuse for a parent. I call her by her name because she doesn't deserve to be called Momma. Gail is the true definition of a junkie. She's a thief, and sells her body just to keep from being sick. I gave up on Gail a long time ago.

I don't know where I would be without my big brother, Markese. He has been my mother, father, and my closest friend. Markese taught me how to walk, ride a bike, and beat a bitch ass if I had to. Markese and his girlfriend Trish spoil me rotten. I want for nothing. Trish and Markese have helped me through all my trials and tribulations. I don't know where I would be without them. Fuck Gail and whoever my deadbeat Daddy is because I know she doesn't know who he is either. I am so ready to get out of Trish and Markese house. They have done enough for me. It's time for me to get my own crib, but I already know that is not about to fly with Markese.

It's summertime in Chicago and there is nothing to do but party and bullshit with my ride or die chick, Niyah. It's going to be hard for me to kick it because Markese be on me. Markese is the HNIC of The Murda Squad, a crew him and his childhood friends started when they were younger. My brother is loved and feared across the city.

Markese and his crew are running shit, and they live up to their name. These niggas are a big part of the reason why the murder rate is at an all-time high. My brother's line of work is dangerous. That's why he tries to keep me out of the hood where he conducts business. That's where he fucked up. Now I hang on the south side of Chicago where they are definitely about that gunplay. I have to be careful about who I hang with and what they know about us. It's kill or be killed on the mean streets of Chicago. People are out here hungry; they're robbing and murking one another left and right. Snitching is also at an all-time high in the Chi, so you definitely need to watch the company you keep.

Markese is always telling me to keep squares out my circle. The same guys that you come up with will be the same ones who will put a bullet in your head, or wear a wire and have your ass facing a life sentence. There is no such thing as loyalty to some people. You have to learn how to separate the real from fake.

Everybody knows that I am Markese's little sister. I can't even have a boyfriend because they're scared of him and the crew. Markese still thinks I am a virgin. Unbeknownst to him, I lost that shit a long time ago. I only deal with men from the Southside because they don't know my brother. It's easier this way.

I listen to my brother though. He has put me up on game when it comes down to dealing with men. . He's always telling me to watch out because all they want is pussy. I'm smarter than that though. There's an AIDS epidemic in the Chi, and I'm definitely not trying to get caught slipping. Markese hates the fact that Trish has groomed me into a bad bitch walking.

At the age of twenty, my confidence is through the roof. I'm a 5'5" red bone, and thicker than a snicker. I got an ass so fat you can sit a drink on it and it won't even spill. I wear all the latest fashions; you would swear I had a job. Markese gives me a monthly allowance and keeps my bank account current.

However, it's time for me to get out and get my own apartment. I want to show Markese and Trish that I can be independent and take care of myself. Quiet as kept, I already found a nice apartment close to downtown in a beautiful area away from the hood.

My girl, Niyah, has been kickin it with this guy named Hassan for a minute now. He and his crew got some major paper. I have never dealt with any of the guys in his crew because they are too disrespectful and ignorant. Hassan is cool as hell though. I can see why my girl is in love with him. Plus, he spoils her rotten.

Hassan has invited us to a welcome home party for his older brother who has been locked up for the past five years. The only thing these niggas have been talking about is the infamous Rahmeek Jones aka *King Rah*. They really be holding this nigga's dick. I don't want to go, but I definitely want to see this man in the flesh.

Niyah and I decided to go shopping at The Water Tower on The Magnificent Mile in downtown Chicago. We found some sexy cream-colored dresses with black heels to match with gold spikes on them. After shopping, we headed over to the salon to get our hair done. I got a blonde bob with a Chinese bang. Niyah got some damn twenty-inch hair weaved into in head. It's damn near one hundred degrees outside! It's too hot for all that hair, but to each its own. We looked good as hell, but why wouldn't we look good? We are from the Westside and we like messing with Southside niggas. It's a known fact around Chicago that Southside bitches can't stand Westside bitches. Therefore, we have to show up, show out, and shut these hoes down. The party is going to be at The Factory Gentlemen's Club, one of the hottest strip clubs in the Chi.

****

The Factory was already packed when we finally got there. Thank God, we were in V.I.P. Hassan had unlimited everything and we blended right in with the crew. I was sipping on Coconut Ciroc and pineapple when the finest specimen I have ever seen walked into V.I.P. I was speechless. Judging from the way everybody was jumping up and hugging him, I knew this was the man of the hour. Rahmeek stood about 6'2" with a caramel complexion, dreads long like Lil Wayne, and a body like Busta Rhymes. Rahmeek was fresh to death in crispy white Air Force Ones and an all-white True Religion outfit. He was the total package and then some. My pussy was soaking wet. I wished I had put on some panties.

"Damn, close your mouth," Niyah said breaking me from my thoughts.

"Niyah, he is fine as fuck," I licked my lips seductively as I watched him work the room.

"Girl, yes! Hassan my baby and all but big bro can get it the long way."

"Naw, don't get greedy. I want this man in the worst way. His name is written all over my Kitty Kat."

We both began laughing. I started getting nervous when I saw Hassan and Rahmeek walking towards us.

"Big Bro, this is my girl, Niyah, and her friend, Aja. This is my brother, Rahmeek."

We both extended our hands and he kissed the back of them. Let me find out Rahmeek is a gentlemen.

"Nice to meet both of you ladies. I have heard so much about you, Niyah but, I'm hurt because I know nothing about you, Ms. Aja."

Rahmeek sat down beside me. I was blushing like a schoolgirl as he whispered in my ear.

"You are the baddest bitch in the room. No disrespect, Lil Momma."

"Thank you, Rahmeek. You're not so bad yourself."

"Where is your man, Aja?"

"I don't have a man," I replied while pouring myself another drink to calm my nerves.

"Well, since you don't have a man, there shouldn't be a problem with me taking you home tonight." He sounded so cocky and sure of himself.

"Boy please, I don't know you like that. What makes you think that I would go home with you?"

"Trust me the wetness between your legs ain't sweat. Only a man of my caliber could have a woman cumming on herself the first time she meets him," Rahmeek said in a cocky tone.

Looking down, I had my legs slightly open. I was embarrassed as hell to say the least.

"Don't worry about it, Lil Momma. He got excited at the thought of you as well."

Both of us looked down at his dick. It was hard and long as hell. This nigga was definitely working with a monster. For the rest of the night, we popped bottles, chilled, and danced so much that my feet were sore as hell. I noticed that Rahmeek was a ladies' man and whispered in a lot of bitches' ears. I was jealous and I didn't even know this man. His confidence was through the roof. He knew he was the shit. That turned me on, but I had to play it cool. Once the club was closed, Niyah and I chilled in the parking lot with Hassan and Rahmeek.

"You going home with me, Lil Momma, or what?" Rahmeek asked.

"No, I'm good. I'll take a rain check, but here is my number. Give me a call so we can get to know each other better."

"Alright, we can do that."

After exchanging numbers, I watched as Rahmeek walked off while wondering if I had made the right decision by not going home with him. Especially since I saw him walking off with that bitch, Karima, who was following him all around like a puppy dog. I can't stand her thirsty ass.

Chapter 2 – Markese

There is no better feeling in this world than riding around smoking on some Kush and sipping on some Remy. I'm on top of the world. I feel like the King of Chicago right now. I got more money than I know what to do with. I remember not having shit while growing up. I dreamt of the day when I would be able to buy anything I wanted, regardless of the price tag. I've been hustling since the age of fourteen. Now I'm thirty years old. Being a hustler is one of the hardest jobs in the world because I risk my life and freedom every day. Fuck a nine to five. I'm my own boss with employees on the clock.

It's killing season in the Chi and everyone is expendable. I'm King around these parts. I'm hated my many, but loved by most. That shit don't bother me one bit. I have been able to stay on top because I give back to the community. It's only right. You can't walk around selling drugs and murking niggas without showing some type of appreciation to the kids or the elderly. My childhood friends, Killa, Mont, Boogie, Nisa, and I have built an untouchable empire. We've been holding court in The Roosevelt Towers since we were shorties. Without them, I am nothing. We are like a family. Besides my crew, I got my two favorite girls in the world; my childhood sweetheart, Trish, and my little sister, Aja. Anyone who fucks with this is signing their own death certificate.

My baby, Trish, is my ride or dies chick. We have been in this shit since we were fourteen years old. Her mother practically raised Aja and me when Gail decided drugs were more important than we were. I wish Trish would marry me. I have proposed several times and each time she turns me down. Trish will not marry me until I get out the game; she refuses to be a drug dealer's widow. Her ass is lucky I love the ground she walks on because I would have left a long time ago. Shit, who am I kidding? Trish will gut my ass like a fish. I most definitely try to tread lightly with her. My sister Aja is my world. I will kill a nigga off site for fucking with her. Niggas know not to let me catch them looking at her. I have no problem with bodying a nigga just for looking. Despite the fact that she is grown, she still needs guidance and stability. I thank God every day for Trish because she is a great role model for Aja. I love Aja with all my heart. I am very overprotective of her. I have to be because niggas ain't shit. Aja deserves to be treated like the queen she is. I am going to make sure she doesn't settle for less.

The Roosevelt Towers make more money in week than most people see in a month, and that's on drugs alone. Not only do we get money from selling drugs, but our murder game is official. When shit gets out of hand, one phone call to the Murda Squad and whatever problem you have will be a distant fucking memory. We don't play games when it comes down to bullshit in The Towers. This is how we eat so I have a very low tolerance for bullshit. We make our money, but we also protect our tenants. There is no such thing as calling CPD when shit goes down in The Towers.

Couples are always beefing in the building, causing a whole lot of commotion and unwanted police presence. Bitches are always beefing over a nigga, so we put a boxing ring in the basement. I'm not with the drama. The last thing I need is for someone to call the police and we have to shut down shop. Why call the police when the Squad is at your disposal?

I got a lot going on in my personal life. Trish is my world, but I have two kids by this chick named Carmen who I've been fucking with for the last five years. I know that I am dead wrong because I love two women. The difference is that I am in love with Trish, and I love Carmen for giving me my seeds. Trish has been pregnant several times, but she can't seem to hold the babies to term. This will break her heart if she ever finds out. That will hurt me because she doesn't deserve to be treated like this.

Chapter 3 - Rahmeek

It feels good to be a free man. I was incarcerated for five years. There are only two things I missed in this world; pussy and getting money. Before I got locked up, I was the motherfucking man. I ran the south side of Chicago alongside my brother. Hassan wasn't able to handle the weight by himself while I was away so we lost our connect. Niggas think we fucked up on the cash, but they don't know that I'm still holding. Prior to going away, I had purchased my first home in beautiful Hoffman Estates that I was sharing with Carmen, the love of my life. I had over ten million in the bank when I left. I thank God that only person who had access to my account was Hassan. Carmen left me high and dry after the first year of my incarceration. I no longer got visits, letters, or anything on the books, not that I needed it. I gave that bitch the world and she just picked up and left my ass. She broke bad on me when I needed her the most.

Since I have been released from prison, I been kicking back and catching up with old business associates. Trying to get back on may be a little harder than I thought. I lot has changed in five years. I already have more money than I know what to do with, but there is always room for more.

I'm glad Hassan gave me a coming home party at The Factory; that bitch was off the chain. I was in a room full of bitches, but only one had my undivided attention. It's been two weeks since I met Aja, and we've been talking on the phone every day.

During our many conversations, I've learned a lot about her. The one thing that stood out is the fact that she is only twenty years old. Aja carries herself like an older woman. I think that's why I am so attracted to her. I was concerned that my age might be an issue for her. I was surprised when she said that she actually liked older men. Once she told me that, I was most definitely going to continue to pursue her. Her ass has been playing hard to get. She surprised me when she agreed to go out on a date with me. I'm taking her to her favorite restaurant, The Grand Lux Café. I offered to pick her up, but she said that she would meet me there instead. When I walked into the restaurant, I observed all the paintings that covered the walls. I searched around the room to see if Aja had arrived. Once I spotted Aja, I just stared at her beauty. Her skin glowed from the way the light hit her face. The red lipstick she had on made her lips look so sexy.

"Hello beautiful. I'm sorry that I'm late. It was hard finding a parking space." Her perfume invaded my nostrils as I embraced her.

"It's cool, boo. I just got here."

"Let's order something to eat. I'm hungry. This is your favorite place. What do you recommend?"

"The shrimp and steak dinner is really good. It's pretty big, so we can share it."

After ordering our food, we ate, drank, and laughed. We enjoyed each other's company for the rest of the night. Sitting there and kicking with Aja, I became even more mesmerized by her. I had to shoot my shot and see if I could get her to come home with me.

"So, what are you doing after we leave here?"

"Nothing. Just going home I'm probably going to watch a movie or something."

"How about you come to my house and we can watch a movie together?"

"Rah, please! You insist on getting me to your house. What do you have up your sleeve Rahmeek?"

"I'm a keep it one hundred with you. You're sexy as fuck and I really want to spend more time with you. I also would love to wake up next to you in the morning."

"Is that so King Rah?"

"I'm so fucking serious, Aja. So, are you coming home with me or not?"

"Yes, Rahmeek, I will come home with you."

I was happy as hell because I thought she was going to say no. I got to have Aja. This girl got my nose wide open and I haven't even had the pussy yet. I hope that tonight I will be able to know what the pussy feels like. I have been the perfect gentleman, but I'm not holding back. Aja is going to have a whole new walk when I get through with her ass.

Chapter 4 - Aja

I can't believe that I agreed to come home with Rahmeek. I was nervous as hell for the entire ride to his house. The only comfort was the fact that he held my hand the entire way to his house. Pulling into his driveway, I noticed the exterior of his house was immaculate. The interior was so beautiful that I was speechless it was lavish as hell. Rahmeek showed me around and told me to make myself at home. He ran some bath water and gave me one of his shirts to walk around in. After I freshened up, I found him in his man cave, smoking a blunt watching the movie *Belly*.

"Why did you start the movie without me?"

"I'm sorry, baby. You want me to start it over?"

"No. I'm good. I haven't really missed anything."

He grabbed my hand and pulled me onto his lap.

"Oh my God, Rahmeek, that Jacuzzi tub was putting me to sleep."

"Yeah, it gets me every time, baby."

Looking into each other's eyes, we got lost in the moment. I leaned in to kiss him. I could taste the Remy and weed as our tongues danced. There was no turning back, so I went all the way. I unbuckled his belt and let his pants fall to the floor. I pulled his boxers down and placed his dick into my mouth. I deep throated his dick . I was trying my best to give him the best head he ever had in his life. I had his toes curling and his eyes rolling in the back of his head. He moaned and groaned as he rubbed his hands through my hair.

"Aja, I'm about to cum."

He tried to pull back so he wouldn't release in my mouth, but I wouldn't let him. I wanted to catch all his seeds. After he came, I pulled my shirt over my head and straddled him. I rode him like a stallion. There was something about those sexy ass lips that I couldn't stop kissing him. After making love in almost every part of the down stairs, I was completely worn out. Rahmeek, on the other hand, was nowhere near finished. He carried me upstairs to his bedroom and we took a shower together. As we laid in the bed, Rahmeek climbed on top of me and placed his dick gently inside of me. His strokes were slow at first but then his strokes became faster. My pussy was dripping wet. I felt like I had pissed on myself. The way Rahmeek was making love to me made me want to cry. He made love to my mind, body, soul, and I loved every minute of it.

 I felt great lying in his California King bed. Rahmeek had drifted off to sleep, but I was wide awake. I just laid there thinking about the night's events. I couldn't wait to call Niyah and tell her about this.

 The next morning, Rahmeek woke me up with breakfast in bed. He had made pancakes, sausage, eggs, and cheese grits.

 "Thank you, but you didn't have to do all this."

 "Of course I did. What type of nigga you think I am?"

 "I don't know, but I'm very impressed."

 "Well this is just a sample of what's to come."

 After eating breakfast we laid in bed for a while longer, I decided to leave because Markese had been blowing up my phone. Markese was probably having a fit because I always answer the phone for him. Rahmeek was definitely worth not answering the phone.

 "Why don't you stay with me for another night?"

 "Baby, I can't stay. I don't have a change of clothes."

"Don't worry about that. My Black Card is on the dresser. I have two cars in the garage you can drive whichever one you want. Go to the mall and shop 'til you drop. You can have whatever you like."

"Are you sure, Rahmeek?"

"I'm positive. I got a couple of moves to make. So, make yourself at home. I'll see you later."

He kissed me and walked out the door.

I couldn't believe he wanted me to stay. Shit, he didn't have to ask me twice. I was still concerned that we're moving too fast, but I decided to take a chance for a change. I've been single for too long, and it feels good being with Rahmeek.

Chapter 5 - Trish

Markese is the best thing that has ever happened to me. We have been together for over fourteen years and are still going strong. He lived next door to me when we were growing up in the projects. My mom knew how bad their living conditions were. My mom loved Markese and Aja like they were her own. She would feed them and allow them to spend as many nights as they wanted. Markese was my best friend until the night I let him take my virginity.

Gail was gone on one of her crack binges again that night. I heard someone knocking at the door. When I opened the door, Markese and Aja were standing there looking pitiful. I hated Gail for doing them like that. I invited them in and laid Aja in the bed.

"Where is Ms. Tina?" Markese asked.

"She had to work the night shift. I'm glad you came over. I was scared in here by myself."

"Let's watch a movie. I'm nowhere near sleepy."

We decided to watch *Straight out of Brooklyn*. I ended up dozing off, but Markese woke me up and told me to go get in the bed. I was so tired I got in my momma's bed. I was surprised when he got in bed with me. One thing led to another then my nightgown was up over my waist and Markese was in between my legs. That shit hurt like hell, but Markese made me feel so damn good. We were fourteen years old and didn't have a clue what we were doing.

From that night on, we made it a habit to have sex every chance we got. My mother never had a clue until I got pregnant. We had to come clean. We had no other choice. Gail didn't give a fuck, but my momma did. She made me get an abortion. Shortly after that, my mom found out she had stage four breast cancer. She died four months after.

I really didn't have any family. Markese and Aja were my family. They moved in with me and we lived like a family. Markese started hustling and was really good at it. At the age of eighteen, he moved us into our own apartment. Fourteen years later, we own our own home.

I own a Hair Salon. I have put my blood, sweat, and tears into making it a success. I spend all my time there while Markese is out hustling. We barely get to see each other, but we live well because we work hard. Since I had the abortion, I haven't been able to hold any babies. I have had three miscarriages in the last four years. I really want to give Markese some kids. I believe that will make us complete.

Lately, Markese has been staying out later and later. I'm starting to get upset about this. Every time I try to talk to him, he says he is out making money. I leave it at that because he has never given me a reason to question his word.

It's three-thirty in the morning and I can't sleep for nothing in the world. I have been calling Markese all day, but he's been sending me straight to voicemail and ignoring my texts. I finally heard the garage door open up and I was about to curse him out. I noticed he was good and drunk when he walked into our bedroom. I had the right mind to slap the shit out of him, but I'm not in the mood to fight his ass. I just gave him that look every man hates to see when he has fucked up.

"Why the fuck are you looking at me like that?" He slurred.

"Really, Markese? You got a lot of nerves asking me that. I have been calling and texting you all day with no response."

"I been busy all day, Trish." Sitting on the edge of the bed Markese began to take his clothes off.

"Busy doing what, Markese?"

"We're not about to play twenty questions. I'm tired as hell."

"Your ass is not tired. You just drunk as hell."

"Trish, please shut the fuck up."

"You shut the fuck up! As a matter of fact, go sleep in the other room."

I pushed Markese out of the bed so hard that he almost fell. "I don't want your drunk ass in my bed.

He stood up and put his finger in my face. "I'm for real. Stop playing with me," he snapped. "Real talk."

I slapped his hand down out of my face. "What you gon' do if I don't?"

"You know what, fuck this shit! I don't want to sleep in here with your grouchy ass anyway. That shit is a big turn off."

"Coming in here acting like a drunk dick is a turn off," I yelled right back.

Markese grabbed the comforter off the bed and went into the guest bedroom to sleep. I didn't have time for his bullshit either. I went right to sleep. I woke up the next morning to his iPhone vibrating on the dresser. My curiosity got the best of me, so I looked at it to see who it was. All I saw were some texts from Killa. As I was about to put it back down, an incoming call flashed across the screen from an unknown caller. I didn't answer. Eventually the caller hung up. . The unknown caller called the phone right back. The phone rang only once. A female voice answered before I could say anything.

"Markese, baby where are you? You're late."

I instantly hung the phone up. My heart was beating so fast and I could barely breathe. Everything around me was moving in slow motion.

I had to sit down to keep from passing out. I have never caught Markese cheating or anything. Not to say that he has never cheated on me he just did a good job of hiding it from me. I guess I got what I was looking for. I couldn't confront him because he would know that I had been in his phone. I placed his phone back down and just crawled back into bed. He came in shortly after and got into bed with me. It took everything inside of me not to bust his shit or cry. He just climbed on top of me and spread my legs apart. I didn't even put up a fight because it felt so good that I had to get into it.

As he made love to me, he whispered in my ear, "I'm sorry, baby. I was tripping last night. I'm sorry for not calling back. I just lost track of time."

My dumbass couldn't do shit but lay there. "It's okay, bae."

After he finished, he took a shower and left. The dick was so good that I was wore out and went back to sleep. I finally got enough strength to get up and get ready for work.

Suddenly, the fact that Markese is cheating on me hit me like a ton of bricks. I need to find out who this mystery woman is. This is my husband. Maybe not on paper, but I got years in this shit. My biggest fear just came to the light and I'm not ready to face it.

Chapter 6 - Markese

I love my baby Trish, and I would never hurt her intentionally. Trish loves me flaws and all. She has been there for me since day one. I been living foul, and the way I been living can be a deal breaker in our relationship. I met Carmen through her father, Juan Rodriquez, who is now my connect. At first, he was against it until he found out she was pregnant with our daughter, Gabriella, who is five years old now. We also have a three-year-old son named Juan. I never intended on getting her pregnant. It just happened. Being a father is the best feeling in the world. I love my seeds more than life itself. Carmen is fully aware of Trish. She knows that Trish is first lady. I make it my business to be active in my kids' lives. I always try to put them to bed at night, but it's getting harder by the day. No one, except the crew, knows about my kids. I feel bad as hell because Aja doesn't even know.

It's Saturday and I promised Carmen that I would spend the day with them. She is starting to get on my nerves, she getting too clingy. Don't get me wrong, Carmen a down ass bitch as well. She's the reason Juan and I are doing business together. Life is good for a nigga like me. Carmen and Trish are well taken care of. I have two of the baddest bitches; I can't even complain. In house pussy and outside pussy comes with perks and pitfalls. I'm getting tired of living a double life. I think it's time to come clean with Trish. On the other hand, I have a date with my kids. They make me forget about all the craziness.

My kids almost knocked me over when I walked into Carmen's house.

"Daddy! Daddy! We missed you," Gabriella said, jumping into my arms.

"I missed you too, Daddy's little princess."

"Hey Daddy, what about me?" Juan said, pulling on my shirt.

"I missed you too, my little Superhero."

Entering the room, Carmen said in a seductive tone, "I missed you too, Daddy."

"Did you cook breakfast?" I ignored her last comment to keep from cursing her ass out.

"Yeah, your plate is in the oven."

"Good. I'm starving. Plus, I need to go to the Towers to see what's popping with Killa."

"No, Markese. Today is family day. You promised."

"I know baby. I'll be back. Plus, I'm spending the night."

"What you gonna tell that bitch, Trish?"

"Hey, watch your mouth. I told you about that shit!"

"Look Markese, I'm getting tired of being the side chick. I'm the mother of your kids. Why you just won't leave her?"

"Bitch, I will never leave Trish, kids or not. You knew what it was from the jump. I got to go. We will talk about this later. You just made me lose my appetite."

"I'm sorry, Markese. Just eat your breakfast. You don't need to be out on an empty stomach."

"I'm good. Tell the kids I'll be back later."

"Yeah whatever." Carmen had a sad look on her face

"Carmen, I promise I'm coming back. Come here." I kissed her on the lips and left.

As I drove to the Towers, I felt like I really needed to get this out. Carmen has been doing too much lately. I need to cut her off. My phone started ringing. It was Juan wanting me to meet him at Nuevo Leon a local Mexican restaurant.

So much for getting up with Killa.

Chapter 7 - Rahmeek

I was happy as hell when Juan agreed to meet with me. I made Juan a lot of fucking money. When I got popped off, I left in good graces. There shouldn't be a problem with him putting me on again.

"Look at you Rahmeek. I see you was in there pumping iron," Juan said hugging me

"There is nothing else to do when you in the joint."

"So, let's get down to why you wanted to meet with me."

"I'm ready to get back on. I'm thinking of starting my operation back up in Gresham Courts, and I would like to start copping from you again. I already know you got the best product in the streets right now. Plus, you know that I'm good for it."

"I don't see any reason why we couldn't start where we left off at. It's ironic that you have come to me with this proposition because I have someone that I would like for you to meet. I'm currently doing business with him, and he reminds me so much of you. He is all about getting money. There is just one thing I have to tell you about him. Carmen has two children with him and they are an item. I'm telling you this because I know the history between you and my daughter. I don't need anything interfering with my money."

"No disrespect, but I don't give two fucks about Carmen or any nigga that she fucks with. What me and Carmen had is over. Far as that man goes, I don't have any issue with him. I'm all about my money as well."

"I just wanted you to be aware of the situation so that I won't regret teaming you two up. Here he comes now."

Looking up, I saw a nigga walking towards us who was iced the fuck out. He had to be an out west nigga. They love flashing their money.

Juan introduced us. "Rahmeek, this is Markese. Markese, this is Rahmeek."

I reached out to shake his hand, but he looked at it and turned his face up, like my hand was covered in dirt. "Naw, bro, I'm good. People don't wash their hands these days."

As soon as those words left his mouth, I was thinking of ways to murk this nigga.

"The reason I wanted you guys to meet is because I think we all can make a whole lot of fucking money if we work as a team. Markese runs Roosevelt Towers, and Rahmeek runs Gresham Courts. Why not team up and shut down the whole fucking city?" Juan said.

"I understand all of that, but I'm trying to work strictly from the Westside. You already know me and my team go hard. We all good on this end," Markese said in a cocky tone. "What he got going on don't have nothing to do with me. Plus, he's a Southside ass nigga and I don't fuck with them period. I'm good only the Squad get money in the Towers."

"Nigga you don't even know me. Plus, I don't fuck with you west side cats. I'm all about my money. As a matter of fact, you can check my background."

"Trust me I already know who you are. I'm not impressed."

"Look both of ya'll just need to calm the fuck down," Juan interrupted us. "This is actually my choice, either your with it or you can cop from someone else. I have plenty of men who are dying to be in your shoes."

"You know what, Juan, I'll hit you later. This shit is crazy," I said.

Markese got me heated talking all that tough shit. That nigga don't even know who the fuck I am. I left the restaurant before the situation escalated. I haven't been out of jail a good month, and this nigga about to have me going back for killing his ass. The only thing that calmed me down was the fact that Aja was waiting for me at my house.

Damn, something smells good, I thought to myself as I walked through my house. As soon as I walked into the kitchen, my dick got hard Aja was sitting on the counter with nothing on but stilettos.

"Do you like what you see, Rahmeek?"

"Like it? Baby I love it."

Aja walked towards me seductively and got down on her knees. She unbuckled my belt and pulled out my dick. With one swift motion, she deep-throated my shit. She looked at me the entire time as she sucked my dick. When a woman is giving you head and look up at you...that shit will make nigga cum quicker than he wanted. Grabbing her hair, I fucked her throat until I came in her mouth and she swallowed all my seeds. I can't believe Aja only twenty and she's a fucking pro at this shit. I pulled her up off the floor and lifted her up onto the island. After the way she had just sucked my dick, I had to return the favor. I spread her legs and dived in, sucking on her clit with no mercy. I fucked her with my tongue while playing with the pussy.

"Oh my God! Rahmeek. Please don't stop baby that shit feels good." Aja bit on her bottom lip.

"You like that, Aja?"

"Yes baby! I'm about to cum!"

I ate Aja's pussy so good that when came, she was shaking like a leaf. I think I saw tears. After gathering herself, she led me up to the bedroom. Aja had all types of kinky shit set up. Lil Momma was with that freaky shit. Laying me down, she blindfolded and straddled me backwards. Aja rode me like a pro. I really underestimated her. I had to show her who was boss though. I instructed Aja to get on all fours and I entered her from behind. I rammed my dick in her pussy and began fucking her with no mercy.

"Oh, Rahmeek, I can feel this shit in my stomach! It feels so good!"

"Whose pussy is this, Aja?"

"Mine."

I slapped Aja on her ass as I thrust in and out of her. "Whose pussy is this, Aja?"

"Yours, Rahmeek! It's all yours, baby."

"What's my motherfucking name?"

"Rahmeek!"

"What's my name?"

"Oh, shit! King Rah."

"Yeah! That's what the fuck I thought."

After fucking for what seemed like hours, we were both exhausted. We just laid there in each other's arms. I usually don't cuddle with a bitch after I fuck her, but Aja wasn't some random bitch. I've never had a woman go to those lengths to please me. She gets brownie points for that shit.

"Rahmeek," Aja said, breaking me from my thoughts.

"Yeah, baby?"

"I don't usually have sex with a man I just met, but I am feeling you."

"I'm feeling you too, baby."

"Can I ask you a question?"

"Baby, you can ask me anything you want to ask me."

"Do you have a girlfriend?"

"As a matter of fact I do."

"Thanks for being honest. If you don't mind me asking, do you love her?"

"I'm actually in love with her."

"Wow, she is one lucky woman."

"No, baby, I'm the lucky one."

"Well I enjoyed you. I'll be leaving in the morning. I don't want your girl to catch me over here and then she gets fucked up."

"Aja, don't you want to know her name."

"I'm cool, boo. That's too much information for me."

"Her name is Aja."

"Boy, I see you got jokes tonight."

"I'm dead fucking serious. You just fucked my brains out with no introduction .You cooked me dinner and treated me like the King I am. I have never had a woman make me feel the way you do, especially at your age. I want to go to bed with you at night and wake up to your beautiful face in the morning. Please move in with me, baby. You won't want for anything."

"I really don't know about this. Everything is moving so fast."

"We both are taking a risk. This is the first time I'm ever doing something shit like this too."

"Okay Rah, I'm in, but I have to tell my brother first. So you have to give me some time."

"Don't have me waiting long, Aja."

"I won't, baby, but while I'm here let's take a shower and eat this dinner I cooked. No funny business in this shower. If we have sex fuck again we will never eat."

"I'm not making any promises."

Aja is the total package. Over dinner, she told me how her brother raised her and still takes care of her. I informed her that now she is my responsibility. I also asked if I could meet her brother. I need to holla at him and let him know there's a new sheriff in town, and I'm not Andy Griffith.

Chapter 8 - Carmen

I can't believe I'm so in love with Markese that I have gotten comfortable with being the side chick. I have stayed quiet about my kids because of the love I have for Markese. It's starting to get the best of me, and I'm definitely losing sleep over this shit. No matter what I do, I will never be enough to make him leave Trish. I have given him the kids she can't and it still doesn't make a difference. When I called his phone this morning, I knew it was Trish who hung up in my face. Markese and I are on good terms so he had no reason to hang up on me. I'm glad she answered his phone. I'm sick and tired of hiding our relationship. I bet that bitch was in shock. Hopefully she cried her poor heart out just like I do every night.

In reality, I know it's not her fault because she doesn't know anything about me. What hurts the most is the fact that he puts her before my kids. It's been five years and nothing has changed. I can't even tell my father about what's going on because he doesn't even give a fuck. He told me from the beginning not to fuck with Markese, but I did anyway. And I'm paying for it.

It's been so long since I have seen or spoke to my father so I was elated when I called and he invited me to have lunch with him. Walking into Nuevo Leon I bumped into none other than Rahmeek "King Rah" Jones.

"Oh my God, Rahmeek, I didn't know you were out. How are you doing?"

"You would know if you would have kept in touch."

"Rahmeek, I'm sorry. I didn't mean to just walk away from you. I just couldn't take being in that big house by myself.

"Bitch, please! You can't give any better excuse than that? At least keep it one hundred If you gon' try to hold a conversation with me. Tell the truth, you left me for that nigga, Markese."

"If you must know, I became pregnant by Markese. How could I come visit you or sleep in your home knowing I was with another man? You would have killed me and him."

"Damn right! As much as I did for you, I should break your fucking jaw right now. You were supposed to be a down ass bitch."

I attempted to touch him, but he yanked away

"Bitch, don't touch me! As a matter of fact, don't even speak when you see me."

Just like that, he walked away. At that point, I realized I made the biggest mistake of my life. Rahmeek gave me the world. Being with him made me so happy. If I could have remained loyal, I wouldn't be going through this bullshit with Markese. I wanted to cry. I lost my appetite. I walked out of the restaurant and went home to drown in my sorrows. I can actually say that I am one miserable woman.

Chapter 9 - Aja

I have been thinking of ways to tell Markese that I'm moving out all day. I have basically been living with Rahmeek since the night we had sex, but I'm not about to tell my brother I'm moving in with him. I might be dick silly, but I'm not brain dead. Since I already paid my security deposit on my condo, it's best for me to keep my own shit. I'm not about to be the type of chick who gets put out of a man's house when I got my own shit. Markese didn't raise no fool. These niggas be in their little moods and don't nobody got time for that.

All I can think about is Rahmeek. His swag is through the roof and he is such a gentleman. Rahmeek caters to my every want, need, and desire. He is spoiling me rotten. He has furnished my entire condo and took me on a shopping spree out of this world. It's more to him than just material things. We are always going out on dates. The Lakefront is our hangout spot where we have picnics and fuck on the sand until the sun comes up. He is so romantic. The thing that really turns me on is the fact that he is one thug ass nigga.

We've been kicking it for about three months now, and I have yet to tell Markese about us. I can tell that Rah is becoming impatient. I know that Rah is a drug dealer. I let him be the man he is and I stay in my lane, like a good wife is supposed to. I don't volunteer information about my brother either. I try not to talk about him. Markese would kill me if I was running off at the mouth.

I've been spending all my time with Rahmeek; that I haven't been able to keep up with my hair appointments. My hair looks a damn mess. Rahmeek keep me on my back so much I can't keep my hair up.

Walking into Trish's shop, I noticed a lot of mean mugging bitches in there as usual. I love being the center of attention. "Hey big sis! What's up?"

"Don't Big Sis me. Where the hell have you been?" Trish asked with her hands on her hips.

"I've been kicking it at Niyah's house."

"Don't lie to me, Aja."

"If I tell you, Trish, you have to promise you won't tell Markese."

"Please! I barely see him to get dick, let alone snitch on your ass."

"Okay then. I met someone and I am really feeling him."

"Oh my God Aja, I am so happy for you. Markese can't trip. You're a grown woman. He needs to understand you are not going to be a little girl forever."

"I'm so scared to tell him, Trish. I don't want him to be mad at me."

At this point, I could not control my emotions. All I could do was cry

"Aja don't cry. I'll go with you when you're ready to tell him. Now wipe your face and give up the goods on this man is that got you sprung."

"Well, his name is Rahmeek. He is thirty years old, and I met him a couple of months ago at a party."

"What's wrong Trish?"

"Damn, Aja, I don't know about this. He's a little too old for you. What did you say his name was again?"

"Rahmeek."

"That name sounds so familiar to me, but never mind that. Are you sure that you're happy?"

"I am so happy being with Rahmeek. He makes me feel so special and so loved. His sex game is award winning. He be having my ass climbing the walls."

"Listen to your little hot pussy ass."

We both started laughing. I can't help it though that man makes my pussy cry like R-Kelly.

Trish's phone started to ring as we were talking.

"Speak of the devil; this is Markese calling me now."

Trish "Hey baby, I'm back here in the office with Aja," Trish said.

Markese entered the office and looked mad as hell.

"Damn, Aja, I been calling your ass all day. Why the hell haven't you been answering your phone?" Markese yelled.

"I'm sorry, Markese. My phone is acting crazy. I'm about to go to T-Mobile and grab a new one."

"That's bullshit and you know it. Since when did you start lying to me?"

"Damn, baby, why you jumping down her throat like that? She is grown as hell!"

"Was I talking to you, Trish?"

"Hell naw, but I'm talking to your ass.

"Trish, you better pipe the fuck down. You been talking real jazzy lately and it's starting to really piss me off!"

"That's the only thing I can do to get your attention, Markese. You already know I do and say whatever I want. Let me get the fuck out of here. I got clients anyway."

"Trish, we're going to finish this conversation at home."

"Nigga please! I'm surprised you know your address. Get the fuck out my office with that bullshit."

"Markese, what the hell is wrong with you and Trish? I have never seen y'all behave like this."

"Fuck that shit Trish is on! What's up baby girl? I miss you so much." Markese hugged me so tight.

"I miss you too, big bro, I have something to tell you."

"I'm all ears, lil sis."

"I met this guy who I am in love with. Before you spazz, hear me out. He is so good to me, Markese, and he spoils me rotten."

"Where he from, Aja"?

"He's from out south."

"No wonder I haven't heard about this."

"Markese, I'm grown now. You can't stop me from falling in love. I have to grow up. That's why I got my own apartment."

"So, you've been hiding all this from me, Aja? This man got your nose so wide open that you keeping secrets from me," Markese raised his voice and I knew he was pissed off.

"Markese, it's not like that. I love you with everything inside of me. No one can ever come between us."

"Why haven't I met him?"

"Because I wanted to tell you about him first."

"Damn, do this nigga have a name?" Markese was yelling at this point.

"His name is Rahmeek." I held my head down because I couldn't look him in the face.

"Come again? The look on his face let me know that there was a problem.

"Rahmeek? Why? Is something wrong?"

Markese stood up and knocked the chair over, scaring me to death.

"Aja are you crazy? That nigga is a drug dealer! He's a thug ass nigga! Not to mention, too old for you. You can end this shit now or I will end his life. I already don't like dude. Of all the people to fall in love with, you had to go and fall in love with Rahmeek's ass."

"What are you talking about Markese? Rahmeek is good to me. Why do I have to stop loving him because you don't like him?"

"Because I said so. He is not good enough for you. End of discussion."

I have never stood up to my brother, but that was about to change. I had to take a stand and fight for my relationship,

"Markese, in case you forgot, I'm a fully grown woman. I appreciate everything you have done for me, but it's time I start making decisions for myself. Rahmeek is who I choose to be with. There is nothing you can do to change my mind."

"Like I said, end it or he is a dead man walking."

"Really? You would do that knowing how I feel about him? I thought I knew you, but obviously, I don't. Never in a million years did I ever think that you would make me choose between you and the man of my dreams."

"I love you more than life itself Aja, but I don't trust Rahmeek. Ever since I had a meeting with him, shit's been fucked up. That nigga didn't get what he wanted so he using you to get to me."

"No he is not! He doesn't even know that you're my brother."

"Bullshit! Don't be a fool! Listen to me and listen to me good…if you value that nigga's life, you will end this ASAP."

"I will not end my relationship with Rahmeek to boost your ego. I mean this with the upmost respect Markese. You walk around like you own the world. You think you have the final say in whatever I do. All this energy you're putting into my relationship, how about you work on yours. Trish loves the ground you walk on and she barely sees you. Go home. Be a man to your woman and stop running my life. On some real shit, go home, Markese. Trish really misses you. I'm moving out tonight. It's time for me to grow up. Please let me do something on my own for a change."

Markese moved closer to me and pointed his finger in my face. "So you're choosing that nigga over me... your family...your own flesh and blood?"

"No. I'm choosing Aja for a change!" I yelled. Markese was so mad that he threw his cell phone up against the wall. "Fuck it. Since you're grown, don't call me for nothing. When he start dogging you out, don't call me. When he gets to whooping your ass, don't call me either."

Tears rolled down my face because my feelings were so hurt. Markese's words were so mean and hurtful.

Markese stood up to leave. Before he left he turned around.

"Oh, yeah don't be out with that nigga when he gets wet up. You might become a casualty of war. Loyalty or death. Remember that shit, Aja." He walked out and slammed the door behind him. I just sat there and cried my poor heart out. I love my brother with everything inside of me. I would never go against him. It was never my intention to fall in love with someone he hates. The comment he made before he walked out felt like a knife in my heart.

I couldn't believe Markese said some shit like that to me. I have been crying ever since I left the shop.

****

I removed all my belongings from their house. Trish cried because she hated what happened between Markese and me. She understood my side of the story, and was pissed at Markese for his behavior. Niyah has been blowing my phone up all night, but I am too upset to talk to anyone. All I want is Rahmeek but he is out handing business .I don't nag him because he is a busy man. He is out doing what he has to do to make a better life for both of us, no matter the means. Rahmeek is my baby. I support him through any and everything.

I'm lying in his bed in complete silence and dark, staring at the ceiling. I'm debating whether or not to tell him about Markese's threats. I decided that I have to because Markese meant it. He don't make idle threats him or them crazy mutherfuckers he run with. I decided to read my latest book, *Rozalyn* by Shan. Reading clears my mind off all the bullshit in my life.

Rahmeek finally made it in the house. I was so happy to see him. I jumped in his arms and cried like somebody killed my ass.

"What's wrong, Aja?"

"I told my brother, Markese, about us. He said that he will kill you if we don't stop messing around."

"Markese? Please tell me you're not talking about Markese from out west."

"Yes, that's him."

"You got to go! It's about to be a war all over your dumb ass not telling me who your brother was."

"I didn't think that it would matter! Please, baby, don't be mad at me."

Rahmeek grabbed me and looked into my eyes. "Baby, it does matter."

"I told him that I love you, and that I'm not going to leave you just because he wants me to."

"Aja, you're really showing your age right now. I don't know what Markese taught you, but the streets don't love nobody. It's money over everything. Ever since I met your brother, we've been beefing. Your brother tried to play me like I'm a lame. If he wants a war, that's exactly what he's going to get."

"What the fuck is wrong with both of you? Y'all really trying to kill each other?"

"Look, this shit between me and you got to end. I can't have you losing your family because of me. Baby, I love you and I have enjoyed each and every moment with you, but shit can get real serious. I don't want you in the middle of this. Now get the fuck out, Aja."

"Rahmeek, you don't mean that. I just lost my brother because I chose you. Please don't do this to me."

I cried and pleaded, but Rahmeek put me out of his house. Luckily, I have my own house. This is the worst day of my life. I lost my brother and the man that I love, all over some bullshit. I cried so much that I made myself sick. I could not keep anything down. I decided to shut everybody out of my life and focus on me. Fuck Markese and Rahmeek! They can kill each other for all I care. Both of these men claim to love me, but when it came down to it, they showed me otherwise.

Chapter 10 - Trish

I seriously can't believe the way Markese has been acting. Lately, he has been snapping and being very disrespectful. I barely see him anymore. Our house feels so empty and broken. There was a time when I was his everything, but now, all he is worried about is getting money and killing Rahmeek. He is so stubborn. He doesn't realize that he is hurting Aja and me with this silly vendetta.

Markese got me fucked up if he thinks I'm going to keep living like this. His ass hasn't been home in a week. He calls every day, all day, like that makes up for his behavior. I deserve better than this bullshit. I have been his down ass bitch since I was fourteen years old. I'm the one that fucked with him when he didn't have shit, not a pot to piss in or a window to throw it out of. I am the one who trapped with this nigga day in and day out. I helped him build his so-called empire. Now this nigga want to try to act all brand new.

He must have forgotten who I am. I can get down with the grimiest of niggas and bitches, but he gone learn today. Since he won't come home, I'm going to see his black ass. I usually never leave the house without my high heels on, but today I'm rocking gym shoes and a jogging suit. It's about to be a rumble in the Towers, especially if he try to front or jump stupid. I have a lot of tension built up inside of me.

Pulling into the parking lot in my burnt orange Charger, I noticed all eyes were on me. These bitches already know when the Queen comes around everything shuts down. As I walked towards the building, I noticed Killa.

"Hey Trish, what's up?" Killa asked, looking suspicious.

"What up Killa? Where the hell is Markese ass at?"

"He's up in his office. Let me hit him up and tell him you down here."

"No, that's ok. I want to surprise his ass."

I pushed Killa out of my way. I think he called himself trying to run interference. All of us have been friends about the same amount of years, but his niggas protect Markese until death. The elevator was taking too long, so I decided to walk up the stairs to the fourth floor where his so-called office was. I banged on the door like I was the police. He opened the door and looked at me like he was pissed.

"What are you doing here, Trish?"

"I came to see why you won't bring your ass home."

"Because I'm handling business. I'm out here getting this money. You know that green shit you like to spend on them expensive purses and shoes."

"Hold on mutherfucker, I got my own money and please don't forget that. All the money in the world won't make up for you not coming home, Markese."

"Trish, pipe down and get out my face before I beat your ass."

"I wish you would put your hands on me. I will tear this bitch up."

"I'm telling you get out of here before I hurt you."

"Hell no! I'm sick and tired of this .You won't come home and you're on a damn rampage with this Rahmeek situation. Not to mention your hurting Aja with your selfish ass."

"Shut the fuck up and mind your business. Aja chose him over me so fuck her."

"Don't ever tell me to mind my business. You need to bring your raggedy disrespectful ass home or you won't have a home to come to!"

"Is that a threat?'

"It's a promise.

Before I knew it, Markese had slapped my ass so hard that my ears were ringing. It was on! I started hitting his ass with my fist and anything else I could find. But he was ready for my ass. He started choking me with so much force that I started to blackout. I looked in his eyes and realized he didn't love me anymore. I have never seen that look in his eyes. Finally, he just dropped me to the floor and I went limp like a ragdoll.

"You happy now, Trish? Ain't that what you wanted...some attention?" Markese was standing over me with his fist balled up.

Slowly getting up off the floor, I gathered my thoughts before I spoke because my mind was all over the place. With tears flowing, I simply told Markese how I felt.

"No. all I wanted was for you to come home. These last couple of months have been hell. We don't go out anymore or do anything romantic. What's the problem? You don't love me anymore? If it's over between us, let me know. I will pack my shit and leave. I'm tired of arguing and fighting with you.

"Trish, you know I love you, but I got a lot going on. I really don't have time to play house with you right now."

"Really Markese? Play house with me? That's how you really feel? After all we been through, that's all you can come up with?"

"On some real shit, I think I need some me time, Trish. I have been thinking long and hard. You can't give me babies, and you won't marry me. It seems to me that you're the selfish one. I need more out of this relationship, baby girl."

I was speechless. Those words made my chest hurt so badly. I walked out feeling like a fool. My intentions were to go over there and bring my man home. Instead, the only man I ever loved treated me like I wasn't shit. It hurt because I really can't have babies for him. I never knew he felt that way.

Chapter 11 - Aja

I was so glad Niyah convinced me to come out and enjoy myself. I was doing just that until Rahmeek and his little girlfriend Karima put on their little show. I'm mad and hurt as hell. I had to play this shit cool though. I swear I wanted to beat her ass for playing with me. There were so many niggas around trying to holler that I had to give Rahmeek a taste of his own medicine. I'm glad I wore my army fatigue summer dress with my matching Michael Kors sandals. My hair was on point as well. I scanned the courtyard until I spotted this dude named Slim that I used to mess around with. Rahmeek got me fucked up. Two can play that game.

I walked over to Slim and gave him the biggest hug ever. Slim palmed my ass and kissed me on the cheek.

"I haven't seen you in so long. How have you been?" I asked, touching his chest.

"I'm good, just getting back in town. I have been away on business, doing what I do best."

"I see you still a busy man."

"You know I'm all about my money, baby. What you doing later?"

"I'm taking my ass home and going to bed. I'm fucked up. You can come scoop me tomorrow though."

Slim and I continued to talk. As we were talking, I felt somebody staring. I noticed Rahmeek shooting me daggers while he was smoking a blunt. Karima was still sitting right there looking like the fool she is. I looked away because I felt like I was doing something wrong. Then reality set in real quick. This nigga just shitted on me for a bum ass female. I kept talking to Slim a while longer. My song, *Blurred Lines,* by Robin Thicke came on and I grabbed Slim. I was dancing on him all seductively while staring at Rahmeek the whole time. I was letting him rub on my ass and everything. I had that Remy in my system and I was cutting up. Before I knew it, Rahmeek snatched me away from Slim's ass.

I yanked away from him so hard that I almost fell. "Rahmeek, get your hands off me!"

"What the fuck you doing, Aja?"

"I'm doing the same thing you doing."

"Your ass is out here acting like a ho, letting that nigga feel all over you!"

"Aww you mad? You're fucking that ho, Karima, so what's your point, Rahmeek? If memory serves me right, you dumped me. Not the other way around. So, please get out my face. I'm not trying to hear that bullshit."

I attempted to walk away from Rahmeek, but he pulled me by my hair and yanked me back towards him. I turned around and tried to slap him. That only made him hold my hair tighter.

"Let my hair go!"

"Don't you ever fucking disrespect me again, Aja. Do you hear me?"

"Yeah, please let my hair go."

Rahmeek finally let my hair go. "Get your ass in the car. I'm taking you home."

I wanted to pop off at him, but the look in his eyes told me to do what he had said.

"I need to tell Niyah that you're taking me home."

"She knows already. Now get in the car."

Before I could get in the car, Slim walked up

"Is everything good, Aja?"

"Yeah, I'm cool."

"Nigga, beat your feet. This ain't got shit to do with you. You had your fun and it's over," Rahmeek said, looking pissed.

"I was talking to Aja." Slim said.

Rahmeek raised his shirt up and showed his gun. "This is my last time telling you. Walk that shit off before you get carried off in a body bag. The choice is yours."

I prayed he walked off and stopped trying to be Captain Save a Hoe. He hesitated for a minute. I was so happy when he walked off. Finally, I got into the car. We were both completely silent so I broke the silence.

"Can I ask you a question?"

"Yeah."

"Are you and Karima together now?"

There was a long silence before he spoke. "She ain't shit to me. She's just something to do when there is nothing to do."

"So, why is she all on your lap?"

"She was trying to make you mad and you fell for the bait."

"What was I supposed to do?"

"You were supposed to act like the lady you are and pay no attention to me or that bitch. Don't ever let anyone bring you down to their level. You are too classy for that."

"Whatever Rahmeek, you're still fucking her."

He never responded to my last comment he just drove me home without saying a word to me. I got out the car and was about to say something, but he drove off without so much as a word. I should have never let Niyah talk me into going to that barbeque.

Chapter 12 – Markese

Ever since Trish and I got into it, I haven't been going home like I should. After the altercation, I went home to apologize for my actions. I walked into our bedroom and Trish was in the bathroom on the floor crying. I really hate myself right now. The things I said to her were way out of line, especially the comment I made about her not giving me any kids. That was dead wrong.

I held my hand out to help Trish up off the floor. "Come on bae, get up."

She pushed my hand away. "Just leave me alone."

"I'm sorry for putting my hands on you and saying that foul shit to you. I have so much going on right now. Plus, your mouth is way too smart. You say shit to make me angry on purpose."

Trish walked past me and sat on the bed. "Whatever Markese. You can keep your apologies. Right about now, it means nothing to me." She wiped the tears from her face.

I sat down on the bed next to her. "Damn, I'm trying to make this shit right between us. What do you want from me, Trish?"

"All I have ever wanted was you .It's sad that you're so caught up in this lifestyle that you have forgotten about me. You can have the money and this lifestyle. I would give it all back just to have you."

I grabbed Trish's face so that I could look into her eyes. "I'm all yours, baby."

"Your mouth is telling me one thing, but your actions show me different. I'm done talking about this whole thing. "

Trish got up and walked out of the room leaving me sitting on the bed. For the rest of the week I tried everything in my power to make up with Trish. I was buying jewelry, flowers, and candy. Trish wouldn't accept anything from me. I got tired of trying, so I just gave up. I was tired of walking around the house not talking to one another. I was also tired of sleeping in the guest bedroom. I haven't been at home that much. I have been at Carmen's house on a regular.

It's been great spending more time with my kids. However, I feel horrible for what I'm doing to Trish. With all that's been going on, I have been neglecting my operation at the Towers. I'm meeting up with the crew to get the latest on what's been going on. The first person I saw when I walked into the building is Killa. This nigga grinds twenty-four seven.

"What's the word 'Kese?"

"Shit, just sliding through checking on things. Where is everybody else?"

"Waiting on you upstairs in the office."

"Okay, let's go up there. I need to run a few things pass them."

"Aye, 'Kese let me holla at you for a minute."

"Yeah, what's up?"

"The relationship you have going on with Carmen isn't a good look. You're walking around with a whole family right up under your girl's nose. All the drama with your personal life is knocking you off your square. Plus, Trish is a good girl. We both know that she don't deserve this.

"With all due respect, Killa. I know you mean well, but my personal life is none of your business."

"No disrespect. I just thought I would let you know you're not on you're A game.

"Can we end this discussion, Dr. Phil?"

"Yeah. I have said my peace."

Killa and I walked into the office and I got down to the business at hand. Killa, Boogie, Nisa, and Mont were sitting around the table.

"What's up 'Kese? You've been M.I.A on us." Nisa said,

"I'm sorry for that I got some shit going on in my life right now."

"It's all good, bro. Let's talk about how we're going to handle this cat, Rahmeek," Boogie said.

"It was one thing for this nigga to fuck with my money, but to find out this man has been fucking my sister, is a whole different thing. She claims that she is in love with him."

"How long have they been messing around?" Killa asked.

"He just got out of jail so it hasn't been that long. He doesn't love Aja. he is just using her to get closer to me."

"Yeah, we definitely got to get at that nigga," Nisa said.

The entire time I was talking, I made a mental note of Mont's behavior. He had a mean mug on his face. It was like he had something he needed to get off his chest. Lately, he has been in his feelings. I need to holla at him later about this.

After catching up with the crew, I had to hurry up and run. Today is my son's birthday party and I have spared no expense. I never had a birthday party as a child so I have to do it real big for my shorties. Juan loves superheroes so I hired all the Marvel Comics Superheroes. Everyone showed up and showed my son love. We had the party at a Community Center because we knew there would be a big turnout.

Trish has been blowing my phone up all day. I was so glad when the party was over because I needed to get home to Trish. After all the guests were gone, I walked out with Carmen, holding Gabriella and Juan's hand. I was smiling from ear to ear until I saw Trish standing was by my car looking at us.

Chapter 13 - Trish

I definitely have been regretting going to the Towers and showing my ass. I'm sure the reason why Markese has been staying away from home is because of that. My heart was hurting so bad from the words Markese spoke to me. We have gotten into arguments and fights throughout our years, but nothing like this. I never confronted him about the woman who called him. There was no reason to. In my heart, I knew he was cheating.

I have been calling him all day with no answer. I was worried so I looked on my iPad and accessed his location on the GPS System that I hooked to his car without his knowledge. I decided to follow him just to see what was more important than me. I followed Markese for about two hours until his location stopped in Oak Park, Illinois. I pulled up and wondered why he was at a community center? I knew he was there because I saw familiar vehicles parked outside.

I sat and waited for him to come out. Finally, he walked out like he was the happiest man on Earth. He was walking with a female that looked like she was Mexican and two kids. My gut told me they were his kids; they were the spitting image of him. Without thinking, I jumped out of my car and all hell broke loose.

"I see why you haven't been home, Markese! Y'all look like a big happy family."

"Damn Trish baby, I'm so sorry. I never meant for you to find out like this."

"Don't you mean that you didn't mean for me to find out at all?"

"Come on kids, let's go," the woman said nervously.

"But Mommy, what about Daddy?" the little girl whined.

"Come on, Gabriella, now."

"Excuse me, sweetie, I didn't get your name."

"I'm Carmen," she stated matter of factly.

"Well, Carmen, I'm Trish, but the look on your face tells me that you already know me. Stay where you are. Don't be in such a rush. I'm not through with you bitch."

"Trish, please let me explain." Markese pleaded.

"Shut the fuck up, Markese! I don't want to hear anything you have to say. I already know whatever we had is over. I have to accept that. It's funny how you're the same one running around talking about loyalty this and loyalty that, but you are the most disloyal person I know. You have a whole family right up under my nose. Does Aja know about this?"

"No, she doesn't know either."

"Well," I snickered. "This just keeps getting better. And you have the nerve to be mad at her for not being loyal. Markese you don't have clue what love or loyalty is."

"Look Trish, it's not that serious," Carmen interjected.

"Bitch, was I talking to you? You're saying my name like we friends or something."

"No, you weren't talking to me, and trust me I don't want to be your friend, Sweetie."

Before I knew it, I snatched her up by that long pretty hair and commenced to kicking on her ass. She thought it was okay to speak to me about my relationship. This ho don't know me. She knows of me and that's the difference. I didn't let that bitch get a lick in. I tore her Mexican pretty ass up. Before I knew it Killa, Mont, Boogie, and Nisa were breaking us up.

"Let me go, Nisa, so I can fuck this bitch up."

"Come on now, Trish, you're too classy for this," Nisa said as she held my arms down. I lost my composure. I just started to scream and shout. I was swinging my arms and tussling, trying to get Nisa to let me go.

"Fuck y'all!" I screamed loudly. "All of you come to my house and sit at my table like family. How could y'all do this to me?"

I screamed and cursed for so long that I was out of breath. All I could do was cry. I wanted to ask Markese how could he do this to me, but I had already embarrassed myself enough. He grabbed me and hugged me to keep me from falling to the ground. I had no more strength. The fight in me was gone. I fell to the ground anyway. Markese picked me up and handed me over to Mont who helped me to my car. Markese didn't even have the heart to walk me to my car himself.

I was in no condition to drive so Markese instructed Mont to take me in his car and would bring my car to the house. The entire ride to my house I cried like a baby. Mont was trying his best to keep focused and drive, but my crying was distracting him. We pulled into my driveway and I was about to get out but, Mont grabbed my arm before I could open the door.

"Trish you are too good of a person to be going through this. I have known you and Markese for a long time and I know you love him. You deserve to be treated like a Queen, nothing less."

"Thanks, Mont." The tears were still flowing heavily.

Mont grabbed my hand and held it. "Come on, Trish, stop crying. You're better than this shit, baby girl.

"How could Markese do this to me?"

"I can't answer that question because I don't know."

I turned around in the seat and faced him. "Mont why you didn't tell me? We have been friends just as long as you and Markese?"

"Trish, you already know I couldn't do that. Plus, on some real shit, it was none of my business."

I looked out the window and wiped the tears from my eyes. "I'm just trying to figure out what have I done, that was so bad to make him hurt me like this."

Mont grabbed my chin and looked into my eyes. "Look, let me know if I'm overstepping my boundaries, but I have to say this. You are a beautiful black woman and you deserve nothing but the best. You don't deserve to be treated like this. Yeah, Markese is my friend and all, but I'm speaking the truth."

"Thanks again, Mont. Let me get in this house."

"Not until you promise me something."

I looked at him curiously. "What's that?"

"If you ever need someone to talk to or need me, you'll let me know."

I nodded my head and got out of his car. I walked into our home and looked at all we had accomplished. What was once my dream house has become the saddest place on Earth. I needed someone to talk to. I didn't want to be by myself. I called Aja several times, but she didn't answer. I left her voicemail telling her to come to the house, because I needed to talk to her. I needed a drink to calm my nerves so I opened up my favorite bottle of wine. I wanted to burn everything Markese owned but that would not help. He would just go out and replace everything.

Two bottles and three hours later, I was drunk as hell and feeling even worse. At that point, I realized I have nothing to live for. I have no family.

I went into my bedroom to find my prescription for Xanax and counted the pills. There were twenty pills. I sat on the edge of the bed holding the pills in my hand. For about an hour, I sat there contemplating if I was truly ready to end it all. I decided I have nothing to live for. Before I took pills, I wrote a letter for Markese and Aja.

Dear Markese and Aja

I'm writing this letter to inform you that I have decided to take my life because life is no longer worth living. Markese, I know that you have always wanted to be a father. That's why I kept trying to get pregnant. I'm sorry for not being able to carry your babies to term. Never in a million years would I think that you would stoop so low as to get another girl pregnant. My heart is crushed. I swear it feels like my soul has left my body. The reason I feel this way is because you are my heart and soul. Today I found out your heart is no longer with me and today I died from a broken heart. I keep trying to figure out what I did to deserve this. Both us know that I have been the best woman I could be. The image of your kids keeps playing in my head over and over again. I'm going crazy at the mere thought that they exist. I have had you to myself for so long, that I don't want to share you with anybody. Not even your kids. Aja, I'm sorry I have to leave so unexpectedly without saying goodbye. Know that I love you with all my heart and I am always with you in spirit.

Love Always,
Trish

With that out of the way, I took the pills and I washed them down with wine. I thought that the pills would work immediately, but they didn't. At this point, I was rummaging through the medicine cabinet, looking for anything that would put me to sleep. Then it hit me Markese always kept a stash of Heroin in our safe. I instantly put the code in and opened the safe up. I removed one of the baggies and closed the safe. I emptied the contents on my nightstand and I snorted all of it. Immediately, my nose began to burn really bad. I felt sick to my stomach, like I had to vomit. I attempted to run to the bathroom, but I vomited on the floor. I lay on bedroom floor unable to move. The effects of the heroin, liquor, and Xanax were kicking in. The room was spinning and I was getting sleepy. I began to drift in and out of consciousness until finally I passed out. It felt like my body was sleep, but my mind was aware of what was going on around me. I could hear Aja's voice.

"Oh my God, Trish! What did you do? Aja screamed.

I heard Aja dialing 911,

"Please, I need an ambulance at 220 E. Lake Shore Drive. My sister is unconsciousness and unresponsive." Please, Trish wake up don't do this to me!" she cried.

Next, she called Markese.

"Markese where are you? Please come home I just found Trish unconscious on the floor! Hurry up! 'Kese. I think she's dying."

"Please, Trish you have to wake up."

The last thing I heard was unfamiliar voices and feeling someone pounding on my chest.

"What did she take?"

"I don't know. I came in and found her like this. Is she going to be okay? Aja asked

"Excuse me ma'am, but we have to get her to the hospital."

Chapter 14 - Carmen

Trish better be lucky my kids were with me. If they weren't, I would have beat the shit out of her. Plus, the bitch caught me off guard. Besides all of that, I'm glad she finally knows. I bet she's somewhere crying her eyes out. Now Markese can be here with his family where he belongs. He simply has no other choice. I know Trish don't want him now.

My kids were so upset about all the arguing and fighting that they cried all the way home. Markese was silent the entire ride back to my house. He wouldn't even look at me. He better not be mad at me for this shit. I wasn't the one acting crazy.

When we got to the house, I could tell some more shit was about to pop off. I put the kids in their rooms because they had seen enough violence for one day. Markese was standing by the island drinking a Corona when I walked into the kitchen.

"Baby, is everything okay? You haven't said a word to me."

"What the fuck you think, Carmen? Trish just found out about this shit. I didn't want her to find out like that. I wanted to tell her myself when the time was right."

"I'm glad she found out. Now we can be a family."

"Are you serious? You and I will never be a family. All we have is kids together, that's it. That's all."

I couldn't help but to laugh at him. "It's funny you say that. This shit has been going on for five years. So, nigga, you're in denial. We are more than just some damn baby momma and baby daddy. Where have you been spending the night at all these weeks?

He drank the rest of his beer and opened up another one.

"I've only been here for my kids."

"Cut the bullshit, Markese! You sleep in my bed."

"What the fuck is your point, Carmen?"

"The point is you been having your cake and eat it too. Now that everything is out in the open your ass can't handle it."

"Bitch, shut the fuck up!"

"You shut the fuck up!"

"I'm about to get the fuck out of here before I hurt you."

Markese tried to leave, but I wouldn't let him. I blocked the doorway.

"Hell naw! You're not going anywhere! We're gonna finish this shit."

"Carmen, get the fuck outta my way. This shit is already finished."

"What you trying to say?"

Markese was so close to me that his nose was almost touching mine. "Bitch what is wrong with you? Do your ass need Hooked on Phonics? I'm done with you. From now on, it's strictly about my kids. Now get the fuck out of my way before I make your ass move."

I refused to move. I couldn't believe this nigga was treating me like a random bitch. Before I knew it, he picked me up and moved me out of the way. I tried to claw his eyes out. He didn't even fight me back. He just threw me on the couch and ran out the door. I didn't even go behind him. I was defeated, and this shit hurts like hell.

I knew that Trish was his woman when I started fucking with him. The crazy part about it was he also treated me like his woman. Naiveté at its best. I guess this is what happens when you fall in love with somebody else's man and have kids with that man.

I have to call this like it really is I was never his woman. I have always been a side chick with main bitch emotions. Now I'm sitting here crying and looking stupid. I have no one to blame but myself. However, Markese's ass is not getting off that easy. He's about to feel my wrath. There is nothing like a woman scorned.

Chapter 15 - Aja

With all that's been going on in my life, I've been staying to myself. I haven't talked to anyone. Rahmeek has not texted or called since the day he dropped me off. Damn, I'm going through it without him in my life. I'm used to being with him every day. This shit is driving me crazy. I'm lonely and sexually frustrated.

Since Rahmeek won't fuck with me, I'm about to make a surprise visit to his house. I'm taking a chance on just popping up at his crib. He might have a bitch over there or anything. I hope not because I will go off. I was nervous as hell as I walked up to his door. My heart was beating so fast. I knocked on the door for about a minute. I turned around and was preparing to leave, when I remembered I still had the spare key he gave me. As soon as I walked in the door, I felt sad because I missed being here. Rahmeek wasn't downstairs so I went up to the bedroom. He was lying across the bed with a towel wrapped around his waist. This nigga looked so fucking good to me. Rahmeek sat up when he realized I was standing in the doorway. The look on his face let me know that he was not happy about me being there. He stood up and walked past me. He stood in front of the mirror and started rubbing scented hair oil in his dreads. I just stood in the middle of the room watching him. He was turning me on by the minute.

"What you doing here, Aja?"

"I just wanted to see you since I haven't heard from you."

"You haven't heard from me because I have been busy. As a matter of fact, I'm about to get dressed. I have to meet up with Hassan."

Rahmeek got up and started to get dressed to leave. I stepped in front of him and dropped my trench coat.

"Aja, you're not playing fair. You know we can't fuck around like that."

"That's what your mouth says, but your dick is saying something else."

I leaned in to kiss Rahmeek on the lips and he kissed me back so passionately. I ripped the towel from his waist. It had been a minute since I seen his perfectly manicured naked body. Our hands began to roam each other's body. He forcibly grabbed my hand and led me to the kitchen. That's our favorite place to get it in at.

This nigga knocked everything off up the table and lifted me up on to it. Rahmeek dived right in and started giving me the business. My ass started to hyperventilate. I couldn't take it. This nigga was eating my pussy so good that I was speaking in tongues. When he got finished, he entered me with so much force that it hurt.

Once the pain subsided, the pleasure set in. After a couple of more rounds in the kitchen, Rahmeek carried me upstairs to the bedroom. We made love for hours and lay there basking in the glory of our love making session. We drifted off to sleep.

****

When I woke up several hours later, I had a bunch of missed calls from Trish so I jumped up and put my clothes on. Rahmeek was sleeping so peacefully so I didn't wake him up. I honestly forgot he said he had to meet up with Hassan.

When I made it to Trish's house, her ass was on the floor. She was unconscious with vomit everywhere. I looked around the room for some clues and found her note. I called the paramedics immediately and then I called Markese to let him know that she tried to commit suicide.

I can't believe this! What the fuck was Trish thinking about? Why would she do this to herself? I know that she and Markese were having problems, but I had no idea it was this bad.

At the hospital, I sat out in the waiting area waiting for the doctors to come out and tell me something. I said a silent prayer for Trish and prayed that God heard me. I needed some air so I decided to step outside and wait for Markese to arrive.

When I exited the Emergency Department doors, I saw a familiar face racing behind the paramedics. It was Rahmeek and he was covered in blood. My heart sank.

"Oh my God, Rahmeek! What happened?"

He pushed me away from him forcefully. "Bitch, get the fuck back."

"What happened? Rahmeek? Please tell me what's wrong?"

"Don't fucking touch me, Aja! This shit is your fucking fault."

I was lost I had no idea what he meant. "What's my fault? Baby, I don't understand?"

"If I wouldn't have been fucking with you, this shit never would have happened."

I attempted to hug him. Instead of hugging me back, he had slapped me so fucking hard that I lost my balance and hit my head on one of the chairs.

"Bitch, don't you ever put your fucking hands on me! Stay the fuck away from me!"

The hospital security tried to go after Rahmeek but, I told them that I was fine. I tried to stand up, but I was dizzy as fuck. I started throwing up everywhere. The security called for a stretcher and I was immediately taking to the back to see a doctor. While I was back there, the doctor asked me a series of questions. There was one question that stood out to me.

"When was your last period?"

I haven't had a period in three months. How could I not realize I didn't have a period? I took the pregnancy test and it confirmed that I was pregnant. After hearing the news, I was in complete shock.

Damn, I'm pregnant by Rahmeek and he doesn't fuck with me. This shit is all Markese's fault. I wanted to cry, but I'm tired of crying. I see why Trish tried to kill herself to get away from all this madness. I gathered myself and went back out to the waiting room to see if Markese had made it.

As soon as I got out there, it was pandemonium! Rahmeek and Markese were fighting like a motherfucker. These niggas was straight humbugging like they were in a boxing ring. The security guards couldn't do shit. I started screaming and hollering for them to stop.

I guess these dumb bitches heard me because they stopped fighting and security held them apart.

"Look, let me tell y'all something with y'all clown asses. This beef y'all got going on has to stop. It's hurting everybody around you. Markese, Trish tried to kill herself because of your selfishness and your ego. Rahmeek, I don't know what happened with you today. I do know this shit with my brother is causing you to treat me like shit. All this shit over money and territory and for what? Y'all are going to be dead and the shit you're fighting over will not be able to go with you. I advise y'all to squash this shit because I'm pregnant with your baby, Rahmeek. I will not bring my child into a family full of chaos. I will leave and never come back."

"If you think telling me you're pregnant is going to make me change my mind about not fucking with you," Rahmeek snickered, "baby girl, you got me fucked up."

Markese ran up on Rahmeek and tried to hit him, but the security guards grabbed him before he could land a punch.

"Nigga, you think I'm a let you dog my little sister out. I don't want you fucking with her no way, but you will take care of your responsibilities. If you think for a minute you gon' be able to walk the streets behind this shit, you're sadly mistaken."

Rahmeek just stood there with this smug look on his face. I didn't want them to fight one another, but I would love for Markese to knock that look off his face.

"Rahmeek, I have come to the conclusion that it's over and you don't want me anymore. You don't have to worry about me or my unborn child."

I guess Markese felt sorry for me because he grabbed me and hugged me.

"Don't worry lil sis. Fuck that nigga. You already know y'all Gucci.

"I know, but get your life right. Until then leave me alone. both of all y'all good for nothing ass niggas need Jesus."

I sat down and waited for the doctor to come out and update us on Trish's condition. As I sat there, my heart was crushed, but I would not let these fools see me cry again. My love for Rahmeek blocks me from feeling sorry for Markese. My loyalty to Markese blocks me from loving the father of my child. Damn, I never thought loyalty or love would be a life changing decision for me.

The doctor came out and interrupted my thoughts. I actually felt bad for treating Markese bad right now. He really needs me more than ever. I got up from where I was sitting and went to console him. Markese had his face buried in his hands. I rubbed his back and he laid his head on my shoulder. I couldn't believe he was crying. I have never, in my twenty years, seen him cry.

"I'm looking for the family of Trish Williams."

Markese jumped up and rushed over to the doctor.

"Please tell me that she is okay," Markese pleaded.

"Ms. Williams took a large amount of Xanax," the doctor explained to Markese and me.

Markese practically slumped to the floor and began to sob uncontrollably. I've never seen him so worried. The doctor attempted to put his hand on his shoulder, but Markese knocked it away.

"Cut the bullshit Doc, how the fuck is my girl doing?" Markese was becoming angry again.

"Sir, we pumped the medication out of Ms. Williams' stomach," the doctor continued. "She is resting and will physically recover from this ordeal rather quickly. However, since this was a suicide attempt, Ms. Williams has been transferred up to the psychiatric ward for evaluation."

Markese got in the doctor's face." What the fuck you mean the psychiatric ward? She is not crazy."

I had to grab him so that he could calm down. The security guards were anxious to put him out of the hospital.

"Ms. Williams has been transferred to that ward because she poses a threat to herself. Her mental state is not good right now. She keeps saying that she has nothing to live for and that we should have let her die."

"When can we see her?" I asked anxiously.

"You can go up and see her now."

"Aja, I can't believe that they have her in the psych ward? My baby is not crazy. She did that shit because of me. I broke her heart Aja. She will never forgive me for this." He started to cry again.

"Yes she will. you just have to give her some time. I promise she will come around."

"I'm about to go see her. Are you coming with me?"

"Go ahead. I'll meet you up there."

I looked over at Rahmeek who was sitting in the waiting area completely distraught with his head in his hands. Despite what Rahmeek had said and done to me, he needs someone to be here for him.

I walked over to him and rubbed my hands through his dreads. He grabbed my waist and cried like a baby. I was surprised he didn't stop me. I wanted to take all his pain away. I feel responsible for this shit. He told me that he needed to meet Hassan, but I just had to get some dick. Hassan and Rahmeek are close as hell. All they have is each other. I sat there with him for about an hour. He wouldn't look at or speak to me. It hurt like hell, but I sucked that shit up. Finally, a different doctor came out of the double doors and asked for the family of Hassan Jones.

"Right here. I'm his brother, Rahmeek Jones."

"I have good news and bad news, Mr. Jones. The good news is that one of the bullets only grazed his head. The bad news is that the bullet that hit him in the neck traveled to the spine area. It's so close to the spine that we can't remove it right now. He is on a ventilator and we have him in a medically induced coma So that he doesn't move and make the bullet shift."

"How long will he be like that?"

"We can't say for sure. He needs to build strength before we can do the surgery."

"Can I go back to see him now?"

"Of course you can."

Rahmeek and I started walking towards the Intensive Care Unit, but he stopped me in my tracks.

"Aja, I'm good from this point. I just can't trust you. You're part of the reason why my little brother is back there fighting for his life."

"Rahmeek, all I can say is I'm sorry. I never meant for any of this to happen. Baby, I love you so much. Please don't treat me like this. We need you," I cried while tears rolled down my face.

"Look Aja, don't cry. It's not good for your baby. I'm so sorry for putting my hands on you earlier. I would never fight a woman. I was just upset."

He walked away just like that. I watched him until he disappeared out of sight. I accepted his apology, but I didn't accept him saying 'your baby' like I'm not carrying his seed.

Reality set in quickly. I'm going to be a single parent because I'm definitely not having an abortion. Since my brother still hadn't come down, I decided to go up and see about Trish. The entire elevator ride up, I thought about how my support system is crumbling.

Pregnancy is supposed to make you happy. Instead, this is by far the saddest day of my life. I rubbed my stomach and told my unborn child that I will always be there for him or her no matter what. My mind drifted off to Gail. It's been a minute since I have seen or talked to her. A girl needs her mother for milestones like this. I don't know why, but I'm going to see her real soon. I just need to put my ill feelings towards her to the side. Lord knows I can't stand her, but I need to forgive her. Life is too short.

Chapter 16 – Carmen

Ever since Markese left my house, I haven't heard from him. He won't answer my phone calls or my texts. I'm starting to feel like this nigga is saying fuck my kids. They could be in danger and he wouldn't even know. He is so caught up with trying to make sure Trish's unstable ass is okay. I heard that she tried to kill herself. I was very disappointed when I heard she wasn't successful. Trish thinks that she is so much better than me, but she's not.

I have no one to talk to. I wish my mother was here. I haven't seen or heard from her since she was deported years ago. My father kept me so sheltered that I never was able to meet people. I wasn't even allowed to go to public school. I was home schooled all my life. My mother never wanted others getting close to me.

Being a part of the Rodriquez family has ruined my life. Maybe if I had had a normal childhood, my adult life wouldn't be so messed up. The only people I have ever been in contact with are the people who deal with my father. That's how I met Rahmeek and Markese.

Despite having kids with Markese, my heart has always been with Rahmeek. He was the first real boyfriend I ever had. What we had was special. When I met him, I already had everything a girl could ask for, but Rahmeek wanted to give me more. He loved me unconditionally, and in return I shitted on him when he got locked up.

I met Markese at my father's house one day. He was so damn cute. His dark skin looked so smooth. He had the perfect set of teeth. He invited me out to dinner and we went out that night. The same night he had me bent over the couch in his stash house. Before I knew it, I was pregnant and had fallen in love with him.

Lately I'm not really feeling any love from him. My father refuses to hear anything I have to say about this entire ordeal. He blames me for Markese leaving. What type of bullshit is that? I have been going crazy without Markese. I can't sleep, eat, or think. Ever since this shit happened, I have been slacking on my motherly duties tremendously.

Rahmeek has been on my mind as well. It's time I pay him a visit. Just thinking about our love making sessions has me feeling all hot and bothered.

The walls of my house are starting to close in on me I need some fresh air. I simply can't get out and explore if I'm stuck with two kids. I'm sick of being a single parent to these kids when they have a fuckin father. Since his bitch ass won't come see his kids, I decided to take them to see his ass. I felt horrible doing this to my kids, but I have to remind this nigga that I didn't have these kids by myself.

"Open this fucking door Markese! I know your bitch ass in there!"

I banged on the door for like ten minutes straight, but I wasn't leaving without proving a point to this nigga and his bitch.

Kneeling down in front of my kids so that we were face to face, I explained to them what was about to happen.

"Look, Gabriella and Juan, Mommy is going to leave y'all here with Daddy for a little while. I promise you that he will open the door in a minute."

"But Mommy I'm scared. Daddy is going to be mad," Gabriella cried

"Shut up, with that damn crying. Be a big girl and watch your brother."

"Mommy, what time will you come back and get us?" Juan asked.

I kissed both of them and told them that I loved them. Just like that, I walked away and left my kids on Markese's doorstep. I'm tired of putting my life on hold for other people. Call me selfish, I really don't give a fuck. I got some major moves to make and I simply can't carry them out with kids in tow. I left and I have no plans on returning anytime soon.

Chapter 17 - Trish

I have been in this hospital for a whole month and I am so ready to get the fuck out of here. The doctors think I am a danger to myself. Ain't shit wrong with me. I'm just a female who couldn't take the fact that her nigga had kids on her. I have been thinking about how I could attempt to take my life when I have my whole life ahead of me. The doctors are telling me it simply wasn't my time to go. The amount of pills I had taken, I should have died instantly. If it wasn't for Aja, I wouldn't be here she saved my life. I was ashamed for what I had done but Aja and Mont have really been a good help with me building my self-confidence. Markese has been trying his best to make me look at the brighter side of things.

Markese has been at the hospital every day since the incident. He will not let me out of his sight. He apologizes every day for everything that he has put me through. At first, I thought it wasn't genuine, but his eyes told me different. I know Markese; his eyes tell his soul. I might sound crazy, but I still love him and I want to try to make it work.

Not right now though. I'm not ready to go back to the house and pretend everything is fine. The doctor came and told me that I can go home today. I'm glad Markese or Aja didn't come because I'm about to get ghost on their asses. I want to be with Markese, but I'm not ready to go home just yet. I have been thinking of places I could go and decided that I should go stay at Mont house. He told me if I ever needed anything to give him a call so I did just that.

Mont picked me up and took me back to his house. I was happy when he told me that I could stay as long as I wanted. I knew I could trust Mont. He wouldn't rat me out to Markese. Markese was about to go crazy because he wouldn't know where I was.

"Trish, make yourself at home. I'm about to run out and grab some food. Do you want anything back?" Mont asked.

"I just need some hygiene products, that's all."

"Look in the bathroom. I keep all those things for my lady friends."

"Wow, that's smart and funny." I couldn't help but laugh at his last statement.

"What's so funny about that?"

"It's just odd that a man would keep things like that in his home."

"I'm not like other men. Once you get to know me, you will see." Mont walked out of the front door.

Mont was going to be gone for a minute so I decided to take a hot bath and a nap. I definitely needed some sleep. You simply can't get any rest in the damn hospital. As I closed my eyes, the first face I saw was Markese. I wondered if I was doing the right thing. I also wondered if Markese is looking for me yet. Knowing his ass, he is going bananas and got the whole team out looking for me. I turned my phones off and my shop remained closed down. I planned on being M.I.A until I got my shit together. I hated doing this to Aja because she needs me. Hopefully ,she will understand my reasons and forgive me for it.

Mont came back about two hours later and brought some Applebee's takeout. We sat at the table and ate in silence. No words were spoken until he asked me a question. It was the one question I was hoping no one would ever ask.

"If you don't mind me asking, why did you try to kill yourself?"

"I was on some drunk shit and I simply couldn't take Markese having kids on me."

Moving the hair from my face, he grabbed my chin, and looked into my eyes. "Ain't no man worth you killing yourself over, baby girl."

At that moment, I saw something in Mont that I had never seen before. I saw his heart. I also noticed how fucking sexy he was. I found myself staring at him and getting turned on at the same time. I had to hurry up and get that thought out of my mind.

"Trish!" Mont said, breaking me from my thoughts. "Are you cool? Is everything okay?"

"Yeah, it's fine. Just zoned out for a minute."

"I'm about to lay it down. Call me if you need anything?" Mont

****

2 weeks later

Ever since I have been here, all I can think about is everything that has transpired these couple of months. Markese's deceitfulness and disrespectful behavior caught up with him and ruined us. I still can't believe that he has kids with another woman. The thought of it makes me sick to my stomach.

Markese had been leaving tons of voicemails on my phone. He sounds like a sad ass puppy. That shit is making me weak because he was actually crying. No matter what he has done, I'm still in love with his trifling, good for nothing, ass. Mont has been the perfect gentleman the entire time I have been here. When he comes I'm going to let him know that I'm ready to go back home to Markese. Shit, I can't keep running from these problems any longer. I need to see Markese, face to face. Call me stupid, dumb, and crazy... it really doesn't matter. I'm going back home to my baby. When Mont got home at about nine with a bottle of Remy and cigarillos, my bags were already packed and ready to go.

"Hey Trish, what's up?" he said.

"Nothing. I was actually waiting for you to come home so we could talk."

"Talk about what?"

"First, thank you so much for hiding me out. It really helped me to clear my mind. I'm going home tonight. Markese is going crazy because he can't find me and I'm going crazy because all I want is him."

"Really Trish? You going back to that nigga after what he did to you?" Mont was so upset with me.

"Yes I am. It's for the best. Plus, I can't hide in your house forever."

"I know that damn. Why don't you wait until morning? You can go home then. The night is young so let's pop this bottle and smoke this Kush."

"Okay, that's what up."

We drank, smoked, and just kicked it. Laughing and reminiscing about the good times we had as teenagers. Before I knew it, I was fucked up and real sleepy. I needed to lay down. I felt like I was about to pass out. I'm not sure what happened, all I know is I woke up naked with Mont on top of me. The crazy thing was that it felt good to me. I wanted more of him. It was like I had popped a pill or something. We were changing positions and everything. All while we were doing it, he kept whispering in my ear. He kept telling me how much he loved me. Something clicked in my mind and I knew I had to get the fuck up and fast.

"I have to go. Markese needs me."

Instantly, Mont jumped up and started going crazy on my ass.

"What the fuck you talking about Markese needs you? That nigga don't even want your ass. You aren't shit but a trophy wife to him. He fucks different bitches all the damn time. Your goofy ass keeps talking about Markese this and that. Fuck that nigga Markese, real talk!"

At this point, I knew this nigga was crazy. I had to get the fuck out of his house and quick. All this damn ranting and raving made me sober up quick. I got up off of the bed to put my clothes on, but he blocked me from leaving.

I tried to walk past him, but he grabbed my arm. "Where the fuck you going, Trish?"

"I'm leaving right now! I should have never come here in the first place. Mont, let me go so I can leave." I tried my best to get away from him, but his grip was strong.

Unexpectedly, he punched me so hard that my nose started leaking instantly

"Your ass not going anywhere until I'm ready for your ass to go. Lay your ass down. I want some more of that pussy."

The look in his eyes let me know to lay my ass back down. I cried the entire time as Mont raped me. The ultimate disrespect came when he made me suck his dick and he came all over my face and took a picture of it. He raped me repeatedly until daylight. He was out cold after awhile. I knew this was my chance to get out of there.

My pussy was throbbing painfully. I barely could walk. I made sure to grab his phone. Markese would never see that disgusting shit. I gathered all my shit and left. I couldn't wait to get home and wash that nigga scent off of me. This shit was all my fault. I had no business being at that man's house. Regardless of us being friends, he was still a man. He plotted this shit. He got me at my weakest point. That nigga built me up to bring my man and me down. After hearing all that shit he said about Markese, I knew he was on something personal. My dumb ass just helped this nigga hurt my man. What the fuck was I thinking?

I cried all the way home. Markese will never want my ass after this. How could I be so fucking stupid and naïve? Driving up to my house, Markese's car was gone. I was glad cause I looked and smelled like a prostitute who been fucking all week and hadn't washed her ass. Walking up to the door, I was in complete and total shock. His damn kids were sleep in front of the door on the ground. I couldn't believe this shit. They looked tired, hungry, and cold.

I kneeled down and gently shook them. "Hey y'all okay?"

"Our Mommy left us all by ourselves," Juan cried

"It's okay. I'm going to call your Daddy right now. Don't cry."

I don't even know these kids' names. I'm mad at the fact that these are his children. I'm even madder that they have been left all alone. I could just break Carmen's neck right now. I needed to get these kids in the house and call Markese to see where he was.

Chapter 18 - Markese

I have been looking everywhere for Trish and she is nowhere to be found. No one has seen or heard from her in two weeks. I got everybody out looking for her ass. I'm hoping and praying that she hasn't hurt herself. This shit is driving me crazy. I can't function. Lately, I've been so off of my square I haven't even spent any time with my kids. Despite all that has happened, I've been making it my priority to get back on my get money shit.

After the fight at the hospital, Juan decided that he would cut me and Rahmeek off completely if we didn't dead the animosity. I definitely don't have time for that. Today we have a meeting with Juan to discuss new business ventures. I'm really not feeling this shit. All I want to do is find my baby. As soon as I got to Juan's house, his head of security led me to his office. Rahmeek was already seated when I entered.

"Markese, my son! I'm glad you could make it. I was just telling Rahmeek how glad I am y'all decided to agree with my proposition. This business venture will bring us in more money than we know what to do with. I also have a side job for you two. I have one of the biggest shipments coming in next week. It's worth of one million dollars. I will be out of town next week, and I only trust you with it. I need y'all to work together on this. No fuck ups. Are we clear?"

"Yeah," Rahmeek and I said in unison.

"Okay, that's a deal. Let's go over all the details."

I left Juan's house quickly after finishing the meeting and getting all the information we needed. I have to get out there and find my baby girl. I have to make this shit right with her. I just hope it's not too late for us.

Killa and me have been smoking, sipping, and riding around looking for Trish and playing Jaheim over and over again

As I rode the streets of the Chi, I thought about this proposition with Rahmeek. He seems to be an alright businessman. On the other hand, it's taking everything inside of me not to kill his ass. He is really treating Aja like shit. On several occasions, I have got at him about the way he's doing her. Each time she tells me to stay out of it, but I can't do that. What type of big brother would I be if I let a nigga treat my sister like this? Aja is putting on a brave front like she's cool, but I know she's hurt. As soon as Rahmeek and I handle this business for Juan, we need to sit down and have a man-to-man conversation. I'm not about to fuck with him if he can't do right by my sister.

I'm glad my crew has been out helping me look for Trish, especially Mont, I really appreciate his help. I have been dodging the shit out of Carmen. I haven't seen her ass since the day I left her house. All I want is my baby back home. I miss lying in bed with her. Hell, I even miss her cursing my ass out.

"My nigga, please don't play this song no more. I swear on everything I love I'm going to help you find your way back," Killa said.

"Man, dog, you think she gone come back?" I passed the blunt to Killa.

"Trish is just mad at you right now. I'm positive she will pop up."

After riding around for a couple of more hours, I realized I had left my phone on silent. I had several missed calls and texts from Trish telling me to come home because of an emergency. My mind was all over the place because, I haven't heard from Trish in weeks. All of sudden out of the blue she calls and tells me that she is at home. Damn, I hope everything was cool with her. I let Killa know what was up and dropped his ass off. I hauled ass trying to get home to Trish. I got the surprise of my life when I walked in the door. Trish was sitting at the table with my kids.

"Daddy, Daddy! Mommy left us by our self and we cried."

"It's okay, Gabriella. I'm here now. Take your brother in the back room and close the door."

"Daddy, are you mad at us too?" Juan asked.

"No son, I'm not mad. Now go with your sister."

After making sure they were gone, I had to turn around and attempt to explain some shit to Trish. I also was curious as to where she has been. I was so happy that she was home. I missed her so much. Trish got up from the table and went in to the living room. I followed behind her.

"Where have you been Trish? I have been looking all over for you."

"I was staying with a friend. I needed to clear my head." Trish held her head down and fidgeted in her seat.

"Are you back for good or do I have to worry about you pulling another vanishing act?"

"I'm here to stay. I did a lot of soul searching while I was gone. I want to try and make this relationship work."

"I'm glad you came back. I was going crazy without you."

I moved closer to her on the couch and kissed her on the lips. Something with Trish was off to me. She refuses to look at me in my face. For some reason I feel like there is more to her just being at a friend's house. Especially since she has no female friends. I'm going to leave it alone for now. My mind drifted back to the fact that my kids were here. I had to try to explain this shit to Trish.

"Look baby, I'm sorry I didn't know that bitch was going to pull a stunt like this. I understand if you don't want them here. I know the kids being here might be too much on you. Just let me make a few calls to see if I can find out where Carmen is."

"Those babies are innocent. They are stuck in the middle of all this bullshit going on. Carmen does not give a fuck about those babies. If she did, she would not have left them on our doorstep. Markese, I love you and I want to be with you. That means I have to love your kids. That's what a real woman is supposed to do. Those kids love you. All they did was talk about their Daddy while you were gone. Markese, they deserve someone to love them and not use them as pieces in a chess game. My love for children would never allow me to mistreat Gabriella or Juan."

"Damn, Trish, I don't know what to say."

"There's nothing to say. Go check on the kids while I take a bath."

Trish had the same song on repeat and was singing along to Tamar Braxton when I walked into the bedroom.

I watched as she sang her heart out with her eyes closed without a care in the world. Looking at her sexy ass made me get rocked up right there. I took off my clothes and got into the bathtub with her. Instantly, she opened her eyes and tried to get out of the tub, but I just held her tighter.

"Trish, baby, just sit down. I missed you so much. I have been going crazy without you. Please don't ever leave like me like that again. I'm not going to ask who you were staying with. It doesn't even matter. The only thing that matters is that you're here now."

After we relaxed in the tub and discussed all of our issues, I made love to Trish over and over again. She was reluctant at first, but I ate her pussy until she cried for me to stop. I made love to her mind, body, and her soul. Lying in bed naked, we heard a faint knock at the door. We put on some clothes and opened the door.

"Daddy, we scared. Can we sleep with you?" Juan said, wiping his eyes.

"No, y'all too big for that."

"It's okay, Markese. Come on y'all."

"Ms. Trish, what happened to your pretty hair?" Gabriella asked.

"Me and your Daddy were wrestling."

"So, that's why I heard you screaming, Ms. Trish?"

We both looked at each other and started laughing. It felt so good having my girl and my kids together under one roof.

Chapter 19 - Rahmeek

It's been two months since Hassan has been in a coma. He has gotten worse since the shooting. The doctors told me that I should prepare myself for the worse. Part of me knows that he can hear me so I will never give up on him. We have been the best of friends since we were young.

We have been in and out of group homes since we were nine and seven. Our mother couldn't take care of us so she dropped us off at the police station. We never saw her again after that. I used to wonder if she thought of us during the holidays or on our birthdays. Our grandmother raised us until the day she died. She did the best she could do with what little she had. I regret giving her hell because there is no telling where we would be if it wasn't for her. She passed away while I was locked up. It hurts me to my heart that I never apologized for the shit I put her through.

My mind is in overdrive because I truly don't know what I am going to do if he dies. Hassan is all I have left in this world. They might as well bury me with him because I won't be able to take it. Niyah has been here every day; talking to him, massaging him, bathing him, and keeping his dreads maintained. I can tell she truly loves him. Not all women can be as loyal like she has to a nigga who could check out any day.

I haven't seen or heard from Aja since the night of the shooting. I think of her constantly. It broke my heart to treat my baby girl like that. I can't believe I hit her. I'm not with that domestic violence shit. I was shocked to find out that she's carrying my seed. I acted like an asshole towards her, but I was going through some shit. I know that's my baby. We never used protection. I've been at the hospital around the clock.

Niyah and I have been alternating schedules. She thinks I don't know that Aja comes up here, but I check the visitor log every day. I can't trip though. They were cool before I even came into the picture.

"What's up, Rah? How is my baby doing today?" Niyah asked.

"Same ol'... same ol'."

"Rahmeek, why don't you go home and get some sleep? I will stay with him tonight. I promise I will call you if anything changes."

"I can't let you do that Niyah. It's my night to stay."

"Go ahead. I insist. I miss him so much that I hate to leave his bedside."

"Let me know if you need anything, Niyah."

"Alright Rah. Be safe. Call me when you make it in."

With that, I left. I'm so fucking tired. I just want to go home and relax. I'm not gonna front. My house empty as hell without Aja being there. Finally, I made it home. I really needed to unwind so I grabbed a bottle of Remy and fired up my Kush blunt in the Jacuzzi. As I took a gulp of my drink and a hard ass pull off my blunt, I closed my eyes and began to relax. My phone began to vibrate. I had a text from Aja. I got my number changed so I couldn't talk to her ass. I know it was that damn Niyah. I hesitated before opening the message.

Hey Rahmeek, I know that you don't want anything to do with me. I just wanted to let you know that I found out we are having a boy.

I replied back.

Oh yeah, that's what up. Congratulations. Have you come up with any names?

King Rahmeek Jones. Do you have any other suggestions, Daddy to be?

That sounds great. Please don't contact me anymore until after you have the baby so I can take a DNA test.

Nigga on my life, you funny as hell. You know damn well this is your baby. I have no problem with giving you a paternity test. I know your trying to hurt me and trust me; you are doing a good job of it. As a matter of fact, fuck you. I regret the day I met your sorry black ass. Me and my son don't need your ass. Know that.

I never got a chance to respond to Aja's last text because a call came through from the hospital telling me I needed to get there as soon as possible.

Damn, I knew I shouldn't have left, I thought to myself as I rushed through traffic.

As soon as I made it there, Niyah told me that Hassan had woke up and they immediately rushed him to surgery. After hours of waiting the surgeon came out came out and informed us that the surgery was a success. The bullet was removed, but Hassan would need rehabilitation to get his mobility back. Both Niyah and I were elated that Hassan came back to us. This whole ordeal has given me a better outlook on life.

After visiting Hassan, I left the hospital and headed straight home. I went straight to my bedroom. To my surprise, I noticed the silhouette of a woman in my bed. All I could think of was Aja and how I was so glad she was there. I climbed into bed and hugged her tight only to find out it was this scandalous ass bitch Carmen.

"Wake up bitch! What the fuck you doing in here?"

"Rahmeek, I missed you so much."

"Bitch, please! You broke bad when I got my time. You done had kids with that nigga Markese and everything."

"I know, but my father thought that it was best for me to move on. I love Markese, but baby, he doesn't make love to me like you do."

"Bitch please! What we had is over and you should not even be here."

"Please Rahmeek, make love to me one more time. I will never bother you again."

Looking at Carmen's naked body and her shaved pussy made me realize I needed to release some tension. I gave her that look to let her know I wanted her to kiss the throne. Just like that, she crawled towards me and removed my dick from my boxers. Slowly she massaged my shaft and placed my entire dick in her mouth. She attempted to make love to my dick, but I had other plans for this grimy ass bitch. Roughly, I grabbed her head and began raping her throat with no mercy. I felt like I about to nut so I pulled out her mouth and sprayed my seeds all in her face. I made her ass turn around and I rammed my dick up her ass and fucked her so hard. The bitch was screaming and squirming trying to get away, but I held on to her until I came. I made sure to hop out. This bitch won't trap me.

"Damn, Rahmeek, you didn't have to treat me like that! You bogus as hell."

"Get the fuck out. Payback's a bitch, you nothing ass hoe."

I put that bitch out my house. She wanted the dick so I gave it to her. I'm a firm believer of the saying *ask and you shall receive.*

Chapter 20 - Markese

The Pick-Up

The boat arrived at the exact time Juan said that it would. Rahmeek and I were standing at the dock waiting for the boat to come in. There were two Mexican men on the boat just like Juan said there would be. As the boat docked, the men handed both of us two black large duffel bags. No words were exchanged between us. We checked the bags to make sure everything was there and it was.

The men pulled away from the dock and we jumped back on the highway to head back to the Chi to stash the heroin at Juan's warehouse. We were about two miles away from the location when we were cut off and surrounded by three black Range Rovers. Six gunmen, wearing all black, exited the vehicles aiming machine guns at us.

"Get the fuck out of the car now!"

"What the fuck is going on?"

Rahmeek reached under the seat. "Just stay calm. I got my gun under my seat, and there is one under yours."

I attempted to reach up under the seat, but one of the gunmen saw me and fired shots in the air.

"Damn, Rah, we're outnumbered!"

One of the gunmen opened the door. "Get out of the fucking car now!"

Both of us slowly exited the car with our hands up in the air.

"Walk away from the car and don't look back!"

We began to walk away from the car, thinking what the fuck we were going to do. The gunmen jumped into the car and drove off with the duffel bags inside.

"Markese, something ain't right. Did you tell anybody about this shipment?"

"Hell naw nigga! Did you? I didn't even tell my crew."

"This shit was a set up. The only people who knew about this were me, you, and Juan," Rahmeek said.

"How the fuck we going to tell Juan we ain't got his shit?"

"We're gonna tell his ass exactly what happened."

Luckily, Rahmeek had his cell phone in his pocket. He called Juan and told him about the robbery. Rahmeek didn't cut any corners. He got straight to the point,

"So you're telling me you don't have my product!" Juan yelled

"Like I said, we got robbed by some masked men."

"Both of you owe me ten million dollars. You have exactly one week to get it to me or there will be consequences."

Juan hung up the phone without giving Rahmeek a chance to respond to his last comment. I was able to hear the whole conversation because Rahmeek had the phone on speaker.

"What the fuck we gon' do now, Rahmeek?"

"We've made Juan some good money over the years. Juan knows that we would never get down on him like that. He has to be behind this shit. Since he want ten million from us, we're about to take everything from him. Get your crew together. We got to plan this takedown. Are you down for this Markese?"

"Hell yeah my nigga! Let's do this shit."

"That's what up. I'm about to call Hassan to come scoop us before we get some unwanted attention."

It took Hassan about thirty minutes to come and pick us up. I was surprised he was able to drive. He was still fucked up from being shot. I had him drop me off at home, but I didn't go inside. I hopped in my car and went to Carmen's house. This bitch has not answered any of my phone calls. I pray she's at home when I get there.

I pulled into the driveway and there was an unfamiliar vehicle parked in the space where I usually park. I made sure I had my gun before I got out. Using my spare key, I entered the house. No one was down stairs so I went up to her bedroom. Standing in the hallway, I could her moans and groans coming from Carmen's bedroom. I opened the door and looked in disbelief. Some nigga was laid back on the bed and she was sucking his dick. I yanked her ass up by the hair and pointed my gun at the nigga

"The party is over, my man. Get your shit and roll out."

"Let me the fuck go! This is my house. He doesn't have to go anywhere."

The guy held his hands up in defeat. "Man, I don't want any problems with you."

I slapped her ass so hard she fell backwards. The dude was so scared that he grabbed his clothes and hauled ass out of the room

"So, this is why you dropped your kids off?"

Carmen got off of the floor and walked in my face." Hell no! I dropped your kids off to you."

"You unfit ass bitch. You left them on the doorstep. Thank God, Trish came home and found them."

"Fuck Trish, I'm so tired of hearing her name!" Carmen screamed.

"No! Fuck you. Who do you think has been taking care of them?"

"She's supposed to take care of them. The bitch should be happy to raise my kids since her insides are all fucked up and rotten and she can't have any kids," she snickered.

I instantly started choking her disrespectful ass. "Bitch, I'm gon' tell you this one time and one time only. Don't you ever play with my kids' lives? Since you're tired of being a parent, you will never see them again. Your ass been gone so long they're calling Trish Momma anyway. Stay the fuck away from me before I kill your ass."

Carmen just looked at me and laughed. It was like choking her gave her some type of satisfaction. I let her go and pushed her on the bed. I walked out of the room and down the stairs.

Carmen came to the top of stairs and yelled. "This shit is not over Markese! believe that. I will be coming for my kids. That bitch is not their mother!"

I didn't even respond to her last words. I had to get the hell out of there before I killed her. I need to keep an eye on her. Carmen is not working with a full deck.

Chapter 21 - Aja

All the bullshit that has been going on has caused me to be very stressed out. This pregnancy has really taken a toll on me. I have lost weight instead of gaining weight. I been on bed rest for the last week and being in the house is driving me crazy. Trish being M.I.A is not helping me either. I'm praying that she is okay.

Markese is driving me crazy. I kinda feel sorry for him. My feelings are so hurt because Markese didn't tell me about having kids. He's dead wrong for that shit. I went off when I found out. I haven't been able to hang with Niyah either because she is taking care of Hassan. I was surprised when she invited me over for Sunday dinner.

Niyah thinks she's slick. I have a strange feeling that she's trying to get me and Rah in the same room. I miss him more than anything in this world, but I don't have time for his shit. Rahmeek is the reason why my son's life is in jeopardy now. I let his bullshit get the best of me. Rahmeek doesn't want to be a part of his son's life, but I have to be in his life. I don't have a choice in the matter.

It's cold outside so I decided to wear my cream and black Akira Poncho with black leggings and my Michael Kors rain boots. I still have to look my best just in case Rahmeek comes. I may feel miserable, but I will never give that nigga the satisfaction of seeing me look miserable.

On the way over to Niyah and Hassan's house, I was nervous as hell. All I could think about was what would happen when I saw Rahmeek. Once I pulled into their driveway, I realized that this wasn't a dinner. It was a damn party. I'm about to kill Niyah! Rahmeek is definitely going to be here! I sat in the car as long as could before putting on my game face and going in. Rahmeek wasn't there when I entered the house. I was relieved that he wasn't there. I walked around until I found Niyah and Hassan in the kitchen.

Niyah ran over to me and hugged me tight. "Hey Aja, I'm so glad you made it! I have missed you so much."

"I missed you too, Niyah! I thought this was dinner. It looks like a party to me."

"It's both. Just relax. You're going to be okay," Niyah said as she checked the food cooking on the stove.

"Hey Hassan, how are you doing big bro?" I asked as I walked over to him and gave him a big hug.

"I'm good. Blessed to be here. I don't know where I would be without my baby."

I noticed that he was walking with a slight limp.

"How is therapy coming along?" I asked.

"Man, that shit is painful! But, I will be out and about real soon."

That's what up! When will the food be ready? We hungry," I said while rubbing my belly.

"Niyah told me you been sick lately. Don't let Rah get to you. He will come around."

Hassan put his arm around me. "I don't think so. He blames me for what happened to you."

"Wow, I didn't know that. I got shot because some broke ass niggas carjacked me."

I gave Hassan a hug because knowing he didn't blame me for him getting shot made me feel a lot better.

Finally, the food was ready so I made my way to the dining area. I saw a few familiar faces from Gresham Courts. Niyah hooked up a wonderful dinner of pot roast with carrots and potatoes, smothered cabbage, baked macaroni, and cornbread. We sat around eating and laughing. It felt good to laugh for a change. Everything was going fine until I noticed Rahmeek coming into the dining room with Karima.

He had the biggest smile on his face and had the nerve to be holding her hand. My smile instantly turned into a frown. Everything inside of me wanted to whoop Karima's ass because she thought she was really doing something. I had to play it cool because my baby was under stress already. Seeing them together hurt my soul, especially since he insisted they weren't together.

I'm pregnant with his son and he has moved on with this Chia Pet looking bitch. This nigga didn't even acknowledge my presence. That hurt my poor heart and soul. I sat there with my game face on, but I was dying on the inside.

They both sat down and started eating like they were a happy couple. The whole scene made me sick to my stomach. Finally, I couldn't take it anymore I excused myself and went to the bathroom. I threw up everything I had eaten all the while crying. A few minutes later, there was a knock at the bathroom door.

"It's me, Niyah. Can I come in, Aja?"

"Yeah, come in."

"Aja, I'm so sorry," Niyah said after closing the door behind her. "I had no idea he would bring that bitch with him. You want me to put that ho out 'cause you know I will. I should go fuck both of them up."

"No, Niyah, it's not necessary. I'm good. Thanks for checking on me though."

"Damn Aja, don't cry. Please don't cry."

"I'm going through hell and he doesn't even care. As a matter of fact, let me get the fuck out of here. Go get my purse and a crowbar. I will leave out the back door," I said, getting up off the floor.

"What the fuck you need a crowbar for, Aja?"

"Stop asking questions. Just go get it and you will see."

As soon as she brought me the crowbar, I walked out the back door around to the front of the house and started busting every window and every headlight in Rahmeek's car. He must have forgotten who the fuck I was!

I drove off when I saw everybody run out. I know how much he loves his cocaine white Range Rover. Fuck him and his truck! I didn't regret that shit, but doing it didn't make me feel any better.

As soon as I made it home, I cried because I couldn't believe Rahmeek had done that to me. I drifted off to sleep, but I woke up because I felt someone's presence in my bedroom. I looked up and saw Rahmeek sitting in a chair at the foot of my bed.

"I should beat your ass for fucking up my truck, Aja." Rahmeek said

"Fuck you and your truck. Get out my house and leave my keys on the kitchen table!"

"I would never put my hands on you again, but watch your mouth, Aja. Real talk."

"What do you want from me, Rahmeek?"

"I came over here to apologize for bringing Karima with me tonight. I was wrong for that shit."

"Rahmeek, I don't care about that bitch. She is a non fucking factor. So don't apologize to me for that. Apologize for the way you have treated me. Do you know what I have been through these last six months? I'm high risk and I have high blood pressure and it's your fault."

"I was bogus as hell for the way I been treating you, but what the fuck you expect?"

"I expect for you to put the baby first. Come to appointments, check on me, and make sure the baby is okay. You don't have to be with me. I have scheduled a DNA test to be done when I give birth to confirm that you are his father."

"I never said I didn't want to be with you or that I wasn't the father."

"You didn't have to say he wasn't yours; you showed me."

Rahmeek sat on the edge of the bed. He tried pulling me onto his arms, but I wasn't feeling him at this moment.

"I'm sorry I've been acting like an asshole. I want to be with you, and I want us to work it out for the baby."

"Rahmeek, that sounds good, but what I'm I suppose to do with you and Markese at each other's head?"

"I have decided to squash the beef. That's the only way we will be a family and make this shit work. Aja, I have done a lot of soul searching and my life ain't worth living if I don't have you or my seed in it."

"Promise me that you won't ever leave us again."

"Aja, I'm not going anywhere and to let you know how serious I am, I'm getting out the game. It's not going to be that easy though. It's hard as hell to get out, but you're worth it. I have something really big planned. After that, I'm done with this shit.

I hugged Rahmeek tight as hell. "Please be careful. I feel like something isn't right."

"You don't have to worry about me. I'm cool. I just want you to focus on the baby and how you're going to pay for my car."

"I'm not paying for shit. That's my payback to your ass for treating me like I was a random ass bitch," I laughed. "Come here and give me a kiss. I missed you so much Rahmeek."

"I missed you too baby." Rahmeek climbed into bed with me and kissed my stomach over and over again. I was happy we made up, but I needed to know a couple of things about his relationship with Karima.

"What's up with you and Karima?

"I'm going to keep it one hundred with you. I have been dealing with Karima off and on over the years. We have been fucking around lately, but that shit is over.

"It better be over. Let that bitch know immediately. I have no plans on sharing you."

"Trust me she already know whatever we had going on is over."

For the rest of the night, we laid in bed and cuddled. It felt so good laying there with him. So many nights I prayed that this moment would return. Our little family is now complete. I can't help but to think about this plan Rahmeek was talking about. I have a strange feeling about it. I don't know what I will do if it Rah gets killed or goes to jail.

Chapter 22 - Markese

I'm happy as hell that Trish is back at home where she belongs. She and the kids are getting along just fine. They actually love being around her. I have been with Trish for quite some time so I know when something ain't right. Trish is not the same person she was before all this bullshit went down. Trish is hiding something from me. I can feel it. That night when we decided to make this shit work, I noticed hickeys on her neck and bite marks on her breasts. I didn't have to ask where they came from. I know she has been with another nigga. I just kept quiet because I wasn't in the position to question her about shit.

I couldn't believe there was another man who had sex with Trish. I know it sounds crazy, but Trish belongs to me. That's my pussy and she had no right to give it away. I broke her out of her virginity and I have always prided myself on the fact that I was the only one she has ever been with. I brought all this on myself. I cheated so she went out and did the same.

Lately, she has been all jumpy and shit. It's like she's scared of me or something. I really need to talk to her. We have been doing great so I should just leave it alone and continue making it up to her. I've been resting and relaxing so I can have a clear head when I meet up with Rahmeek. Plus this shit with Juan got a nigga on pins and needles. He is really threatening us. I can't wait until we get his ass. After all these years of working with him, I never thought it would come to this.

Carmen hasn't attempted to contact me. I can't wrap my mind around the fact that she just left her kids. What type of mother is she? They have been asking about her every day. I just keep telling them that she will be back. How can I tell my kids their mother is a selfish bitch and don't give a fuck about them?

Lying in the bed, I heard Trish in the bathroom on the phone whispering. I got up to listen at the door.

"Please stop calling me and threatening me. I love Markese. What happened between us was wrong."

Trish sounded like she was crying. She became silent so the person on the other end had to be responding to what she just had said. I prayed I was dreaming, but her next statement let me know that I wasn't dreaming.

"Yeah, I'll meet you with the money, but I can't do this anymore. Markese is starting to get suspicious."

After hearing her say this, I was pissed the fuckoff. I wanted to break her fucking neck. I got back in bed and pretended to be sleep. I had my eyes slightly open. I watched her as she came out the bathroom crying. She went straight to our wall safe and took out some of my hard-earned money. I couldn't believe Trish was taking money from our household and giving it away.

"Markese."

"Yeah." I said trying to sound like I was sleep.

"I'm about to go to the mall and grab a couple of items. I'll be back later."

I sat up in bed and started putting my shoes on. "That's a good idea. I'll go with you."

"No, baby, that's alright. Get you some rest. I will be back shortly." Trish walked over to the bed and kissed me. It took everything inside of me not to lay hands on her ass. I watched as she walked out the front door, to give my money to someone else.

As soon as Trish left, I grabbed my keys and followed her. My heart was hurting because she's letting somebody extort her out of money. Trish knows that I will kill for her, and she didn't even come to me for help. My pride is definitely hurt.

I was curious to know who the fuck had the balls to fuck with my girl. I followed her for about thirty minutes. She was driving fast as hell. I almost lost her, but I was able to keep up with her. The route that she was taking was very familiar to me. I began to fear the worst when I saw her pull into Mont's driveway.

I parked a way's down so that she couldn't see me. I was still close enough to see the front of the house. Immediately, my hurt turned into anger and rage. Trish walked up to Mont and handed this nigga the money she took from my safe. He grabbed her ass and attempted to kiss her on the lips, but she turned away. I took my gun out of the glove compartment and took the safety off. I was about to get out and murder both of their disloyal asses. I quickly changed my mind. I couldn't kill them in broad day light. Plus, I wanted to holla at Trish first. I need to know why she did this to me.

I was more disappointed in Mont. he is one of my best friends. I have to know why he doing this to me as well. I know he doesn't need the money. So, what's his point of taking money from my girl? Lately, he has been acting like a real bitch; whining about us hooking up with Rahmeek. It really don't matter why he doing this. I'm definitely putting a bullet in his head.

I want to kill them so bad right now, but I have to wait this one out. I already got beef with Juan and now I got beef with a nigga I break bread with. I left because I had to clear my head. This was some embarrassing shit. I didn't want the crew knowing about this.

    I went back to our crib to wait on her. I went straight to my man cave and opened up a fifth of Remy. I drank it straight from the bottle. That shit was so strong my insides burned. I fired up a blunt and went into the living room. I wanted her to see me as soon as she walked in the door. I sat my gun on my lap and continued to drink while smoking my blunt. Trish is going to tell me what the fuck is going on tonight, or else I'm going to kill her and throw her body in Lake Michigan.

Chapter 23 - Trish

This shit has got to stop and now. So far, I have given Mont almost $500,000 of Markese's money. It's been a month since Mont started blackmailing me. When he first called me asking for money, I flat out refused. That was until he sent a package to my shop. I opened it up and there was a DVD inside. There were instructions for me to watch it and call him afterwards. I watched it and all I could do was cry.

I couldn't believe that he had been videotaping me the entire time I was at his house. I hated myself for going to his house in the first place. After watching the tape, I called him and that was the first time I met him to give him money. I knew I should have told Markese right then, but the images on the tape were too embarrassing.

Markese has been trying so hard to make things right. I have fallen in love with his kids. Our life has been going so good. How could I ruin everything? Ever since I left Mont's house I have been crying all the way home. I prayed Markese was gone when I made it back. I had no such luck.

"Markese, baby, where are you?" I called while I walked through the house looking for him.

"I'm right here."

I turned on the living room light and Markese was sitting there with his gun in his lap. "Why the hell you sitting in the dark?"

"Where have you been, Trish?" He had this crazy look in his eyes. He was drinking straight from the Remy bottle.

"I told you I was going to the mall."

He sat the bottle down and took a pull from his blunt. "What did you buy?"

"They didn't have anything I liked."

Markese stood up with his gun out and moved closer to me. I could tell he was drunk. He had that look in his eyes that scared the shit out of me.

"I'm gonna ask your ass again, and I want the truth," he said slowly, his menacing eyes were boring a hole into my soul. "Where the fuck you been?"

Oh my God he knows, I thought to myself. I was silent as I stared at my man like a deer in headlights.

"Markese," I stammered. "Please don't do this. I can't tell you-"

I didn't get a chance to finish my plea because Markese punched me in my mouth. He just started beating me like I was a nigga in the street. Punch after punch, kick after kick, all over my body, my head, and my face. I fell to the floor and curled into a ball. I knew that both of my eyes were going to be black when this was all over.

"How long you been fucking Mont and giving him my money?" Markese picked me up and body slamming me back onto the floor.

My body was in so much pain. I felt like he had broken every bone in my body.

"It only happened once when I was staying there."

"Bitch, you mean to tell me while I was out looking for your ass, you and that nigga were laid up?"

Markese started to whooping my ass some more.

"It wasn't like that!" I screamed. "He raped me and now keeps asking for more and more money." I was trying my best to explain to him.

"How much of my money have you given this nigga?"

"I'm not sure. I'm so sorry, Markese! You have to believe me. I never meant for this to happen."

I grabbing on to his pants leg and held on for dear life. He yanked his me off of his leg with so much force that I fell back and hit my head on the coffee table.

"Bitch please! You were at the nigga's house. What the fuck did you think was going to happen? Get your trifling ass up."

Markese grabbed me by my hair and dragged me upstairs.

"Take off all your fucking clothes. Bitch you better not come out this bathroom until you scrub all that nigga's dirt off of you."

"Markese, please stop. You have to let me explain." I begged and pleaded for him to stop.

"Shut the fuck up and strip. You like to be a ho, I should treat your skank ass like one. Stop all that damn crying. You weren't crying when you were hiding out from me!"

I slowly took off all my clothes. I stepped into the shower and turned the water on. There were so many cuts and bruises on my body that it stung when the water hit them. I cried harder as the water poured over me. I cried because the water hurt. I cried because I brought this on myself. I should have just told him what was going on. Now it looks like I was in on this shit. Markese sat on the toilet and watched me like hawk with his gun still in his hand.

"Did you suck that nigga's dick, Trish?"

"No Markese."

Markese walked over to the shower, opened the curtain, and slapped me across my face.

"Bitch, you lying!"

"No I'm not Markese." I had to put my hands up in front of my face to block the blows.

"Bitch, you disgust me right now. I can't stand to look at you or touch you. So much for us getting back on track. You know he's a dead man, right? I got the right mind to kill your ass right now. That will have to wait though. You gonna get my money back from that nigga first.

"Markese, please don't make me do this."

"Bitch, shut the fuck up and get out this shower before I beat your ass again."

I did as Markese told me to do because my eyes were already swollen shut. I could feel it. I was praying this ass whooping was over. I definitely know how Tina felt when Ike was tagging that ass. I could barely see, let alone walk. Markese eyeballed me as I tried to walk past him. He snatched me up by my throat and slammed me on the bed.

"If you ever in your life cross me for another nigga, I will kill your ass. Do you hear me?"

I nodded my head because he had me around the throat so tight that I couldn't speak.

"You are not to leave this house without my permission. I don't want you talking to anyone about this, not even Aja."

"Okay."

Markese released me and grabbed his car keys off of the nightstand. "Where you going?" I cried.

"Oh yeah, don't speak to me unless I speak to you. Just get yourself prepared to get my fucking money back."

He walked out of our bedroom. I heard the front door slam and his car leaving out of the garage.

I cried myself to sleep because this shit was far from over. When I woke up, my body felt like a ton of bricks. I could barely move. When I looked at the clock, I realized I had slept the entire day away. I was in so much pain that my ribs felt like they were broken. It hurt like hell to breathe. I finally got the strength to get out of the bed. After limping into the bathroom, I was horrified when I looked in the mirror.

Both of my eyes were black and bloodshot red. My lips were swollen and so was my nose. Markese had ripped my hair out by the roots. Clumps of it were all over the floor. I had bald spots all over my head. I mustered up the strength to go downstairs to get some ice for my lips and some witch hazel for my eyes. I heard the TV on in the living room. I knew that meant he was in there. I tried to move around as quietly as possible. Markese would probably want to whoop my ass some more if I breathed the wrong way.

I got what I needed and went back upstairs and got back in bed. Not too long after that, I felt Markese come into the bedroom. I pretended to be asleep. This nigga was itching to tag my ass some more, I could feel it.

Markese climbed into bed and pulled the covers off of me with so much force that I flinched. All I could do was cry quietly. I slowly got up to walk out of the room, but I felt sick to my stomach. I rushed to the bathroom. I was vomiting everywhere which hurt my ribs even more.

"What the fuck you throwing up for, Trish?"

"I think it's because I haven't eaten anything." I got up off the floor and flushed the toilet.

I got up off the floor and went to brush my teeth. The light was still off so Markese still hadn't seen my face. He cut the light on and I can tell he didn't expect to see my face that fucked up. He hurried up and cut the light off. I walked passed him to go into the other bedroom, making sure not to make any eye contact.

"Where the fuck you going, Trish?"

"I'm going to sleep in the other bedroom."

"Get your ass in this bed now!" He raised his voice so loud that I jumped.

I made an about face quick as hell. I have never been scared of Markese until now. I really believe this nigga wants to kill me. I can't say he's wrong for what he did to me. I'm dead wrong for going M.I.A on him. I should have just stayed and handled the situation like a woman. I was flat out wrong for confiding in Mont. I had no business being in that man's house. I should have told Markese the moment he started extorting money from me. I kept a secret to save my own ass, and now I'm paying dearly for it. We both laid there in the dark. I knew he was awake.

"Markese, do you hate me?"

"I hate your fucking guts right now. Imma say this again...don't say shit to me unless I say something to you."

That hurt worse than him whooping my ass did. I have to get his money back. I have to regain his trust and show my loyalty to him.

Chapter 24 – Rahmeek

Now that my personal life is back in order and I got my girl back, it's time that Markese and I handle this situation with Juan. I'm glad we put our differences to the side and decided to link up. Some shit is just not adding up. No one knew about that shipment but us. I'm not the smartest mutherfucker, but something in my gut tells me that Juan is behind this.

We are finally having the meeting today to discuss our plans. We are meeting up at my warehouse. I'm glad everybody made it on time and I was glad. I needed to get back home to Aja. This pregnancy has her clingy and hungry as hell.

"I just want to say thank you for coming. I know that this is a transition for both sides to link up. But all of our lives are in danger if we don't handle our fucking business ASAP."

"I'm not sure what the fuck is going on so fill me in," Killa said.

"A couple of weeks back we made a pick up for Juan. In the process of dropping the package off, we were robbed at gunpoint," Markese said.

"Damn, what Juan talking about?" Nisa said, looking concerned.

"We got two weeks left to get him his money or we're dead. That's why I wanted y'all here. I believe Juan is behind all of this," Rahmeek said.

"Wait a minute! That's his own shit though?" Hassan said.

"Not exactly. Juan is our connect, but he gets the product from his older brother, Hector, in Colombia. He has to pay a percentage of whatever he makes to his brother. I guess Juan wanted to be greedy so he robbed us so he wouldn't have to pay him. Now because we were robbed, we owe him and Hector."

"Juan ain't got nothing but dough. I do not understand why he would do this?" Boogie asked.

"Greed, pure and simple." Markese stated.

"So, what's the plan, Rahmeek?" Killa said.

"Since he want to rob us we gon', rob and murk his ass first. He threatened my family and for that, his old ass got to go. Me and Markese gon' call him and tell him we got his money. While we're meeting up with him in his office, y'all will be downstairs robbing him for his money and product."

"So, check it out. I already know y'all murder game is official. Not to toot my own horn, but I got a couple of bodies under my belt as well. I know for a fact that he keeps all his money and drugs in an underground tunnel beneath his house. This is where our work comes in. I have been able to put his head of security on my payroll. He has informed me that there are cameras all over the fucking place. He will power them off when we get there. He also gave me a layout of the entire house. Nisa, I need you to come out of gangster mode for one night. He has all types of security at the front gate. I need for you to put on your sexiest gear. I want you to act like your car broke down up the road and you need to use their phone because your cell phone died on you. If that nigga wants to feel on your ass, let him. If he wants to fuck, you get that nigga naked and blow his fucking brains out. Can you do that for us?"

"Man, Rahmeek, I got to put on a dress? It's cool though. I will take one for the team. Let's get this money, but y'all owe me."

"Hassan, Killa, and Boogie, this the most important part of the plan. While we are taking the old man out of his misery, y'all will be outside waiting for Nisa's cue that the coast is clear. Y'all will be posted at the back of the house. As soon as y'all enter the back door, there is a pantry with stairs which leads to the tunnel. Get in and get out. I want that bitch empty. Don't worry about me and Markese. We will hold off on killing Juan until y'all give us the cue that you got the dope and are gone. We have to be on point. No fuck ups or we die. We going in as a team and coming out as family. We're not losing anybody. We're going in alive and we coming out alive.

"Does anybody have questions or doubts? Speak now or forever hold your peace."

Everyone agreed to the plan. I was happy because that money will have all of us looking real nice for a long time.

"Okay. This shit goes down next week. We all need to get rest and be focused. Oh yeah, we're moving the girls to a safe place."

With that being said, everyone got up to leave the room and Hassan showed them out.

"Aye, Markese, can I holler at you on some personal shit?"

"Yeah what's up?"

"If you don't mind me asking, where is your boy Mont at?"

"Mont won't be a part of this operation. He is no longer a part of this crew," Markese stated matter of factly.

"Good. I don't trust that nigga. His eyes tell me he a snake. I also wanted to talk to you about Aja."

"What about her?"

"Look, I know that you don't want me with Aja, but we are trying to build a family together. I know I hurt her by not fucking with her when I first found out she was carrying my seed, but I was real salty about Hassan. Every day I'm trying to make it up to her. I plan on spending the rest of my life with her. So, basically I wanted to know could I get your blessings to ask for her hand in marriage."

"Aja means the world to me besides my girl and my seeds. She is all I that I have. She's a grown woman who is about to be a mother. I'll give you my blessing under one condition."

"What's that?"

"That you protect her and never put her in harm's way. Rah, she loves you so much that she stopped fucking with me, so all I have to say is love her, and if you ever hurt her again that's your ass, nigga."

"Yeah, yeah nigga I know. But, don't tell her I'm going to propose. She doesn't know yet."

"I got you Rah. Now let's get this fucking money."

We dapped each other up and parted ways.

Chapter 25- Aja

I have been calling Trish for the last week and I have yet to speak to her ass. She doesn't even know how things are going with Rahmeek and me. Markese hasn't been answering his phone either. Some shit is going on and I'm about to find out.

I pulled up to their house and saw Trish's car in the driveway. I knew she was home, but all the lights were out. That's not sitting well with me because she hates the dark. I looked into my purse and found my keys. I entered the house and it was eerily quiet.

"Trish, where are you? I know you're here so answer me!"

"I'm up here in my room Aja."

Trish's room was pitch black. "Damn cut on the light. What's going on? I've been calling you. Why aren't you answering the phone?"

I hit the light switch and was horrified at the sight of my sister-in-law.

"Oh my God! What the fuck happened to you, Trish?" I was in total shock and disbelief.

"I'm okay. It's better now, Aja."

"Who did this to you?"

Trish turned away without looking at me and I knew Markese did it. My brother is not a woman beater, so I'm confused right now.

"What the fuck is going on? I can't believe this shit. Markese beat you like this? I'm about to call his ass right now."

"It's all my fault, Aja. I betrayed him in the worst way. He doesn't love or want me anymore. I brought this all on myself."

"Trish, I don't care what the fuck you did. He didn't have to do you like this. Please fill me in because I'm lost."

"Aja, when y'all were looking for me, I was staying with Mont. I was only there as a friend, but he had a hidden agenda. While I was there, he raped me and videotaped me. Now he's blackmailing me. I've been giving him Markese's money to keep quiet. Somehow, Markese found out and beat my ass. I deserved it. He said I have to get his money back, but I don't know how to do that. I need your help, Aja. Please help me. I love Markese. You have to believe me."

Trish fell into my arms and cried her eyes out. I felt sorry for her because I know she loves my brother, but I also had to give her a piece of my mind.

"On some real shit, I know you love my brother. That shit you did was dead wrong. You lucky he didn't kill your ass. You need to get it together. Laying in this house feeling sorry for yourself will not make this situation better. Get up and fix yourself up. We're about to get this money back."

"How are we going to do that, Aja?"

"We gon' get it back ourselves. All we need is Nisa and Niyah to help us."

"Aja no! Markese doesn't want anybody to know about this, not even you. Nisa or Niyah can't know."

"Look, you can trust Nisa and Niyah. We gon' do this shit, and we gone do it right. We fuck with goons and we are their ride or die chicks. When one of us hurt, we all hurt. We about to set it the fuck off."

"You are six months pregnant. Rahmeek and Markese will kill me if something happens to you behind my bullshit."

"Let me worry about all of that. Now get up and get ready I'm about to call the girls over here."

"Thanks Aja. I really appreciate this."

"You've been helping me since forever. It's time I pay you back."

Two hours later, Nisa and Niyah had finally arrived.

"Daammmnnnnnnn!" They both sounded like Smokey from Friday.

"What the fuck happened to you?" Nisa said.

Trish went on to explain to Nisa and Niyah about the whole situation.

"So, this explains why Markese is in a bad fucking mood. Oh my God! Y'all, this shit is happening at a bad time. We have some major shit going on y'all.

"I'm so sorry Nisa. If I could handle this shit myself I would," Trish said.

"I can't believe Mont is doing this! We supposed to be a family. Fuck that shit! Mont is a dead nigga walking."

"Yes, he got to go. I don't want him nowhere around this family. I'm ready to kill his ass right now." Aja said.

"Rah and Markese will kill me if they knew I was plotting this shit with y'all. I love y'all like the sisters I never had. If we gon' do this, it has to be ASAP. I have to be ready for this job I have to do with the team." Nisa said

Trish's phone started to ring. She picked it up and glanced at the caller ID.

"Oh my God! This is Mont calling my phone now," Trish said, looking scared.

"Answer it and put it on speakerphone," Niyah said.

"Yeah bitch, Imma a need $10,000 from your skank ass."

"Look Mont, I can't give you anymore of Markese's money."

"Fuck that nigga! I'm not trying to hear that unless you want his bitch ass to see the videotape!"

"No, no I will give it to you. Where do you want me to meet you?"

"At my house and wear something sexy. Be here by eleven tonight."

I hung up the phone and threw it across the bed. "This shit is crazy. I can't do this y'all."

"Oh, yes you can, and you will meet up with him. Act like you trying to fuck that nigga. We gon' be right outside waiting for you. You gon' drug his ass just like he did you," Nisa said.

"I pray this shit works," I said, sounding skeptical.

"I do this shit for a living ladies. Just follow my lead and nothing will go wrong."

We went on to plan the night out. I prayed we got out without any fuckups. My brother or Trish don't deserve this from Mont. Murking this nigga is going to feel good as hell.

Chapter 26 - Trish

I'm nervous as hell about this whole situation. I'm so nervous that I'm constantly going to the bedroom. I put on my all black cat suit with my all black leather thigh high boots. I put foundation on to hide the bruises on my face. I hopped in my car and called Mont to let him know that I was on my way. The girls followed me to his house but parked down the block.

"It's about time you made it, Trish." Mont said, hugging me.

"I had to wait until Markese left the house."

I took off my coat and his eyes got big as saucers.

"I see you took my advice and wore something sexy. You're looking good enough to eat."

"I've been thinking. Being with you would probably be a good thing since Markese no longer wants to be with me."

"It's about time you realized that. Now come over here and show Daddy how much you missed him.

I straddled him and began kissing him. I let him get all into it so that I could distract him. He never saw seen the needle coming until he felt the pain in his neck. I injected him with a drug that made him unable to move, but he would be able to feel pain. I wanted him to be fully aware of what was about to happen. I let the girls in and we immediately went to work on him. We stripped Mont naked and tied him up. When he came to, he had four familiar faces standing around him in all black with guns drawn.

"What the fuck? What the hell did you do to me?"

He attempted to move, but quickly realized he was tied up. He just started panicking.

"Shut the fuck up! I heard you like to rape females," Nisa said, hitting him in the face with the butt of her gun causing teeth to fly from his mouth.

"Aargh! Aargh," Mont screamed out in pain

"Didn't she say shut the fuck up?" Aja asked before shooting him in both legs.

"Y'all bitches crazy!"

"Bitch? Who you calling a bitch?"

Niyah spit her razor from her mouth and climbed onto Mont's lap. She began carving the word rapist into his chest as he hollered in pain.

"Stop all that damn hollering! Your ass wasn't hollering while you were raping me."

I pulled my secret weapon out of my purse. After everything he put me through, I had to torture his ass. I pulled out the meat grinder, placed his dick and balls into it, and slowly turned the handle.

"Where the fuck is my man's money?"

He managed to let out a slight whimper with some words. "I ain't telling you bitches shit."

"Oh you're not?"

I began to squeeze harder and harder. Finally, he couldn't take any more. He pointed towards the closet. I squeezed his dick until blood shot out from it. His ass was alive but barely. In the closet, we found a secret door that led to another room. We were shocked at what we had found. This nigga had surveillance on everybody. Our comings and goings, drug transactions...everything. Mont had enough to put his whole crew away for a long time.

"We have to burn this bitch down now! Grab the dough and let's be out," Nisa said.

After we grabbed the money, we started pouring gasoline all over the house. I made sure to pour some on his ass. I wanted Mont to suffer. I was glad the girls were there to help.

After striking a match, we walked out of the house with the house in flames behind us. I felt such an adrenaline rush go through my body. Before going our separate ways, we made a pact to never speak on what we had just done. I had to hurry up and get home before Markese, considering the fact that I'm not supposed to be outside.

Chapter 27 - Markese

I haven't slept a wink since all this bullshit been going on. I feel real bad about putting my hands on Trish. My emotions and my ego got the best of me. I can't even look at her so I've been avoiding her. I stay out real late and leave early in the morning. I hope and pray that her face heals. I will never be able to forgive myself if it doesn't.

Ever since Carmen left our kids, Trish has been a hell of a mother to them. I'm glad they weren't home when all of that shit happened. Right now, I have them out in the guesthouse with our nanny, Rosario. I can't have them looking at Trish while her face is looking like that. I checked on them before going in the house with Trish.

Something smells good as hell, I thought to myself as I walked into the kitchen.

"What you cooking this time of night, Trish?"

"I had a taste for some chicken. There's enough for you if you want some."

She grabbed a plate and put some chicken on it for me. Trish handed me the plate and walked out of the kitchen. I wanted to follow her, but I know she's still scared of me. After eating the chicken, I went upstairs to our room to find money all over our bed. Trish was in the shower so I went into the bathroom.

"Why the hell is money all over the bed?" I startled her by yelling.

"I got your money back."

I stepped into the shower and closed the shower curtain.

"How did you get it back? Did you have to fuck to get it back?"

"No Markese. I got your money back plus some. I fucked up and I had to make up for it. Does it matter how I got it back?"

"As a matter of fact it does, Trish."

"Well I'm not going to tell you. If you want to beat my ass again, then so be it. I deserve it anyway."

She walked out of the bathroom past me. Grabbing her arm, I turned her around looking her into her eyes.

"You didn't deserve shit. I should have walked away like a real man is supposed to. I'm sorry. I will never put my hands on you again."

Trish hugged and kissed me. I lifted her up and laid her on top of all the money on the bed. I made to love to her all night and apologized over and over again. She was crying and apologizing as well.

The next morning Rosario brought the kids over and we all ate breakfast. I turned on the TV to watch the news. BREAKING NEWS flashed across the screen as a reporter began to speak.

"A five alarm blaze that has been burning for at least six hours at a house in Oak Park, Illinois has finally been extinguished. Fire fighters searched the house and found what they believe to be the body of the homeowner, Lamont Wilson. Due to the presence of an accelerant and trauma to the body, this is being labeled a homicide."

I knew Trish was behind this. I know I told Trish to get my money back, but I wanted to kill that nigga myself. Trish was just sitting there with her poker face on.

"Do you know anything about this?"

"Who me?" She pointed to herself. "You told me I couldn't leave the house. I have been here the whole time."

"Pack y'all a few bags," I said. "We're going away for a little while."

"Come on kids were going on a trip." Trish was smiling the entire time.

While Trish was packing, the doorbell rang. It was the mailman. He had a small package addressed to me with no return address. I opened the package. It was a DVD without any writing on it. I walked into the theater room, placed the DVD into the player, and pressed PLAY.

The very first thing I saw was Trish dressing and undressing in a room, unaware that she is being watched. The next scene was of Mont and Trish drinking on the couch. Trish never saw Mont slip a mickey in her drink. Eventually, she passed out. Mont checked to see if she was out cold. He started to violate her in the worst way. Mont undressed her and carried her to his bedroom.

Mont got on top of her and spread her legs. As soon as he entered her, she jumped. It looked like she was enjoying it for a minute, but snapped out of it. Mont started snapping and breaking shit in the room. Trish was scared as hell. I saw it in her eyes. The next scenes were so graphic and disgusting that all the life drained from my body. This nigga savagely raped her and purposely took pictures and videotaped the shit to get back at me.

I never knew Mont felt this kind of way about me. I ain't never did shit but be a friend to him, and he's been against me all this time. How could I miss all the signs?

Tears began to fall from eyes because I knew that Trish didn't fuck him willingly. All she kept saying was 'I have to get home to Markese.' Mont hated that shit. Trish probably would never look at me the same, not after the way I whooped her ass. I was about to cut the DVD off, but Carmen's face popped up on the screen.

"That bitch ain't so perfect now, is she? It's funny that you always try to uphold this bitch like she the Queen of Sheba. She ain't shit but a ho who ran to your friend's house just to get away from your no good, lying, cheating ass. This is so hilarious to me. I guess you're regretting the fact that you left me because she found out about our affair. Let me rephrase that...I mean our relationship. We were together for five years. That's not an affair. Oh, yeah, how does it feel to be a single parent? It's a shame I had to leave them on your doorstep, but what was I supposed to do? You wouldn't answer the phone for me, and you wouldn't come see them. Drastic times call for drastic measures. I will be back to get my kids, Markese. Please believe that shit. It's a shame I have to do all of this to get your attention. I bet I got your undivided attention now. You are going to regret the day you shitted on me. Ain't no fun when I got the gun, motherfucker. Now watch me work and watch closely. Oh yeah, one more thing. I bet it killed your soul to see your bitch sucking your friend's dick. You better hide your guns because that bi-polar bitch might try to blow her brains out this time."

Carmen has lost her mind. She and Mont have been plotting against us for a while, obviously. Mont is at the morgue and this bitch is on the loose. I have to put a bullet in her skull ASAP. My emotions are everywhere. I gathered my thoughts and destroyed the DVD. I have to keep this shit to myself. Trish will never know that I saw it. I wish I could kill that nigga Mont all over again for doing my baby like that.

"Markese, we're ready to go," Trish said, breaking me from my thoughts.

"Alright, baby." I hugged her tight and gave her a kiss

After dropping Trish off, I went to The Towers to find the crew. As I pulled into the parking lot, I saw them standing there. The look in their eyes let me know that they had heard about Mont.

"Markese, what the fuck is going on? They're saying it was a homicide," Boogie said, sounding pissed off.

"Yeah, that's the same shit I heard on the news."

"Who the fuck would want to kill Mont? They know he's a part of our crew. I know he's been on some bitch shit lately, but we're still a family," Killa said.

"Family don't hurt family," Nisa said as she walked away and got into her car.

We were speechless as we watched Nisa drive off. Her comment meant one of two things; Nisa knows who did it or she did it herself. The look she gave me let me know she knew what had happened. Nisa had helped Trish get my money back. I knew she hadn't told Killa and Boogie. My pride and my ego would never let me tell them what happened between Mont and Trish. That shit was too embarrassing. Hopefully, this don't come back and haunt us later. I'm taking this to my grave.

Chapter 28 - Markese

The Takedown

We've been sitting in Juan's conference room on pins and needles, praying the crew got all the dope. As soon as we made it to Juan's, we handed him two duffel bags full of money. This nigga wanted to count the money by hand to make sure it was all there. This was great because it gave the crew more time. As soon as we got the word from the crew that they had the dope and were out, it was time for us finish this shit.

"I'm impressed," Juan said. "I didn't think you would be able to come up with the money."

"Cut the bullshit, Juan," Rahmeek said. "We have made you a substantial amount of money over the years. Obviously you're low on cash since you had to snake us to get this."

"How dare you come into my home and insult me! You fucked up the pickup and you have to pay for that. Now get the fuck out of my office before I blow both of your fucking brains out." Juan stood up and pointed his gun at us.

At that moment, we instantly upped our guns and had them pointed at him. Before we could even let off a shot, Carmen and the five masked gunmen who had robbed us walked into the conference room.

"Why wasn't I informed about this little party?" Carmen said.

"*Mija,* what are you doing? Who the fuck are these men?" Juan asked angrily.

"Don't *mija* me! Your ass has never been a father to me."

"Carmen, what the fuck are you doing? Get your little crew out of here because before they be some dead motherfuckers," Rahmeek said

"I suggest you shut the fuck up, Rahmeek. There is no room for your ass to even be talking me. I'm still having hard time dealing with the fact that you raped me."

"Bitch please! You were begging for the dick so I gave it to you. You and I both know I don't have to take no pussy."

"*Mija*, talk to me what is all this about," Juan interrupted.

"This is about all of you," Carmen sneered. "First, you are the worst father in the world. How could you sit back and allow these men to hurt me and your grandchildren? It's all about money with you and these two clowns. Second, Rahmeek, yes I left you high and dry when you were locked up. I needed more than you were able to give me. Regardless of all that, I did love you. Expecting me to wait for you was selfish as hell. Last but not least, the father of my children. Markese, you know this is all your fault right? All I ever wanted was you, and all you ever wanted was her. You just left my kids like they weren't shit."

I cut her ass off. I didn't want to hear it. "Save all that crying! You're the one that left your kids on my fucking doorstep like they weren't shit. Trish is more of a mother to them than you will ever be."

"Markese, fuck you and that dick sucking bitch." Carmen wore a sinister smile on her face.

That bitch really struck a nerve within me and she knew it.

"*Mija*, please put the gun down. Let's talk about this. I'm so sorry. I didn't know you were feeling this way.

"Yeah, listen to your father and put the gun down," Rahmeek said

"My father? Please. This is what I think of my father."

Carmen turned around and shot Juan twice in the chest. We knew we had to get the fuck out of there. Gunfire erupted all over the room. When the smoke cleared, the gunmen were dead and so was Juan.

Carmen was gone, and Rahmeek was on the floor with a gunshot wound to the chest.

Looking up, I saw Nisa and Killa in the room with their guns still smoking. They looked just like Bonnie and Clyde. I was happy as hell to see them. We needed to get Rahmeek to the hospital quickly. We made a call to Hassan and Boogie and told them to me us at the hospital.

Rahmeek is big as hell. It took everything inside of us to drag him out the house and into the car. We kept talking to him, trying to keep him alert, but he was drifting in and out of consciousness. I drove him to the nearest hospital I could find, but he had to be air lifted to Cook County due to the trauma.

They rushed Rah to emergency surgery immediately. He had lost a lot of blood. Hassan was able to donate blood to his brother. Thank God, Killa and Nisa stayed behind just in case some shit went wrong. Rahmeek and I would probably be dead if they hadn't. We sat in silence, just waiting it out to see if he was going to make it.

My crew informed me that the drugs and money were secured in our storage units. I was relieved about that. First thing in the morning, we will be taking the money to our accountant to clean it up. It's time for me to call the girls and break the news. Aja is going to kill me if Rahmeek doesn't make it.

After informing the girls of what happened, I felt like shit, they were all screaming and crying. I even teared up because I know my sister loves that nigga. Man, Rah has to pull through this.

Finally, the doctor entered the family room and told us that the surgery was successful. The bullet had missed his heart by an inch and exited through his back missing vital organs. Our quick actions saved his life.

Rahmeek was in recovery and would remain in the Intensive Care Unit. He was in a medically induced coma so he could heal. The girls finally made it to the hospital and were relieved when they found out he would be okay. We all decided to leave to get some much needed rest. Aja stayed with him. With everything that was going on, I got a good look at Nisa. I was feeling the way she looked. From the look in Killa's eyes, he was feeling her too.

Chapter 29- Carmen

I have been contemplating ways to get back and both Rahmeek and Markese but I couldn't think of anything. That was until I paid a visit to my father. Since I have been a little girl, my father has always discussed business in front of me. Sitting in his office, he went into detail with his head of security about a big shipment that was coming in. That's how I found out that Markese and Rahmeek were going to do the pickup for my father. It was then that I came up with the idea to rob them. My father would instantly think they stole from him. I prayed that he would kill them. I was trying to find some people to pull off the robbery for me.

One night I went to the bar. I saw Mont while I was there. We began drinking and talking. The more we drank, the more we expressed our hatred for Markese and Rahmeek. I took a chance and told him my plans. He agreed to help me. He hired some young thugs to do the actual robbery. We were both lonely that night. So, I went home with him. One thing led to another and we ended up having sex. While I was there, he showed me the videotape of Trish. That shit made my day. I begged him to let me send it to Markese, with a message attached.

The robbery was a success. We split the money among us and the gunmen. My father told me about what had happened with shipment. He was convinced that Rahmeek and Markese were behind the robbery. He informed me that they were coming to drop off the money they owed him. I informed Mont and we were supposed to meet up at my father's house. Our intentions were to rob my father's cellar and kill all of them.

The morning we were supposed to carry out our plan, Mont went M.I.A on me. We were going to use the same gunmen we used for the first robbery. When I entered my father's office, my emotions got the best of me. That's what knocked me off my square. As soon as I shot my father, I regretted it. Gunfire erupted all around me. I had to think fast. Then I remembered my father's secret door in his office that led down to the cellar.

I got the shock of my life when I realized the cellar had been completely cleaned out. My father's head of security was dead. Whoever did it tortured his ass. His throat was slit from ear to ear and his dick had been cut off. Blood was everywhere. I felt a pain in my stomach and realized that I had been shot. I guess the adrenaline caused me not realize the pain before.

I was starting to become weak and feel pain. I used all the strength I had to get the fuck out of the house. I needed to get to the hospital quick. As I climbed up the stairs, I didn't hear anyone so the coast was clear. I walked out the back door and got into one of my father's cars. I was attempting to drive myself to the hospital when all of sudden I started to lose consciousness. The next thing I know I hit a tree head on.

Two weeks later

"Welcome back, Ms. Rodriquez. You have been out for quite some time," a lady said to me.

I was having a hard time focusing. My throat was so dry. "Where am I?"

"You're in the hospital, Ms. Rodriquez. You were in an accident. You have been in a coma for two weeks. I'm Nurse Green and I have been caring for you since you came here."

My mind started to race. I was trying to remember what happened to me. It took me a minute, and then everything came back to me. I started to pull at the tubes and the IV that was in my arm. I had to get out there immediately. If Rahmeek and Markese knew where I was, they would kill me. All the moving around I was doing caused pain in my stomach.

"Oh, no. Ms. Rodriquez. You are in no condition to leave. "

The nurse fixed my tubes and reinserted my IV into my arm. I think she put something in the IV because I drifted off to sleep. I wasn't sure of how long I had been sleep. When I woke up, there were two detectives in my room. They were investigating my attempted murder and my father's murder.

"Ms. Rodriquez, I'm Detective Mike Jordan. I'm sorry to bother you at this time, but we really need to ask you some questions. Do you think you're up to it?"

The detective was clean cut and very handsome. His demeanor made me comfortable enough to speak with him.

"Yeah, I think I can do it."

"Do you know who killed your father and who shot you?"

"Yes, Rahmeek Jones and Markese Jackson."

"Do you have any idea why they would do this?"

"They owed my father ten million dollars. They didn't want to pay him so they set him up. I just happened to be checking on my father because we are so close. I was just at the wrong place at the wrong time." I purposely made tears come from my eyes.

"Calm down, Ms. Rodriquez. Everything will be just fine. Are you willing to sign a statement and testify in court? That's the only way we will be able to convict them."

"Yes, sir. I loved my father so much. They deserve to pay for this. The only thing is I fear for my life. They are vicious drug dealers and Rahmeek is a rapist. You have to put me in witness protection. They will kill me if you don't."

"I don't see that being a problem. You will have to sign an agreement saying that you will testify. After that, we will begin making arrangements to have you moved to an undisclosed location."

"Thank you so much."

The detective came off as being concerned at first but, then his questioning became harsh. If I didn't know any better, I would think that he was working for them. His line of questioning turned into an interrogation.

These niggas thought this shit was over, but they were wrong. The only way this vendetta will end is if I'm dead or in jail. Markese deserves everything that happens to him. He was out cheating, making babies, and living a double life. He not only hurt Trish, but he hurt me as well. He has caused me to turn into the side chick from hell. He had no idea who he was fucking with. I'm one crazy bitch.

It has been a month since I was placed into protective custody. They have me way out in some hick ass town that's probably not on the map. I am going crazy being here. I have no phone or a computer. This shit really sucks. I was happy they had some cool agents watching me. I felt safe with them. I was glad I no longer had to deal Detective Jordan. He was really getting on my last nerve. He kept asking me the same questions about Markese and Rahmeek. I told him a thousand times that I am sure they did it, and I don't know why.

    I was able to lie about this with a straight face. I couldn't give him an inkling that I'm on some bullshit. He ain't a rookie. He's a seasoned vet. I will be glad to testify against their ass, but that isn't happening anytime soon. As far as I know, they haven't even been arrested yet. But the cops assure me that they will be. I can't wait. Their asses gon be buried under the jail when I get through with them.

Chapter 30 – Aja

I'm so fucking happy right now. I have finally made it to my third trimester. Today is my baby shower and Rahmeek is being released from the hospital today. I swear I love that man with all my heart and soul. Rahmeek came into my life unexpectedly and swept me off my feet. Now I'm pregnant with his son and my life couldn't be any better. I truly cannot believe that we have become one big happy family.

All the decorations have been hung and I'm just waiting for the guests to arrive. Markese and Trish went to pick up Rahmeek from the hospital. He doesn't want me doing anything until the baby arrives. I was so happy to see Rahmeek when he finally made it to the house. He looked fine as usual. I wanted to tell everybody to go home so I could fuck his brains out, but we couldn't have sex because he was still in so much pain.

The whole crew sat around enjoying one another, eating, and toasting to the good life. I received so many gifts that the whole house was filled up. The team definitely showed up and showed out. Markese and Trish are in competition with Niyah and Hassan to see who will be the godparents. These fools out here opening up college bank accounts already. It's hard for me to choose so they are both the godparents. I'll wait to tell them. I get a kick out of them arguing.

I was leaning against Rahmeek while he rubbed my belly when I felt him get tense for no reason. Before I could ask what was wrong, my front door was kicked in and police, in full body armor and guns blazing, came storming into our house.

"Police! Everybody get down now!"

"Man, she's pregnant! She can't get down." Rahmeek yelled as most of my guests hit the ground.

"Do you have a fucking search warrant?" I asked.

One of the officers threw some papers at me. My blood froze when I picked them up off the floor and read over them.

"There's your search warrant!" the cop sneered. "And the arrest warrant for Rahmeek Jones and Markese Jackson."

"Get the fuck out of here with that bullshit. What the fuck we getting arrested for?"

"Shut the fuck up! Y'all are under arrest for the murder of Juan Rodriquez and the attempted murder of Carmen Rodriquez. Cuff their asses! As a matter of fact handcuff them all and take them to the precinct."

"Wait a minute!" I yelled. "My niece and nephew are upstairs and you can see I'm pregnant! I can't go to jail!"

"The kids will be going into DCFS custody if no one is able to pick them up by morning. And pregnant or not, you're going to jail," the cop laughed. "No one told you to hang around with thugs."

At that moment, Rahmeek and Markese got away from the officers because they hadn't been fully handcuffed and they start kicking that officer ass for talking shit. All the police started beating them down with their fists and billy clubs. All I could do was cry as they handcuffed us and they took us to jail. Before we left, I saw the cops tearing our house up.

At the precinct, the women were separated from the men and they put us in a holding cell. Trish, Niyah, and I sat next to each other, crying and praying for a miracle. I can't believe this shit.

Chapter 31 - Trish

One Month Later

My life has drastically changed over the course of a couple of months. I tried to kill myself. I killed Mont, and now I'm a stepmother to kids I never knew existed. Just a minute ago, I was the baddest bitch walking. Now I'm looking like the little old lady in the shoe. This shit is tragic.

Since Markese is locked up, I have to take care of the kids because they don't have either one of their parents. It's hard as hell. Every time I look at them, I am reminded of his infidelity. I love those babies though. I have gotten attached to them. I would never do anything to hurt them. On the other hand, their mother is a dead bitch when I catch her.

I have so many emotions inside me. I miss him. I love him. I hate him. I'm scared without him. On a happier note, I just found out that I'm pregnant. I'm not too happy about it though. Today I'm going to surprise him and visit him. I just finished doing my hair and putting on a cute outfit that's suitable to wear.

I was so nervous on my way to the jail because I don't know what his reaction will be regards to my pregnancy. I waited for what seemed like forever and finally it was my turn to visit. The correctional officer brought my baby out and I lost my composure. I cried like a baby. Markese looked like he had the weight of the world on his shoulders.

"Baby, don't cry. I need for you to be strong for me right now."

"I know," I said as I wiped my eyes. "I've been trying to be strong, but seeing you just made me realize how much I miss you."

"I miss you and the kids, but don't worry, I'll be home soon. I promise."

"Don't do that, Markese. Don't make promises you know you can't keep."

"Look Trish, I'm getting the fuck out of here baby. Don't ever doubt your man. I'm coming home to my family."

"Okay baby"

"How are the kids doing?"

"They are a handful and spoiled rotten. Juan and Gabriella have become so attached to me that I can't go to the bathroom without them looking for me."

"Trish, I'm so sorry that I'm putting you through all this. I know it's hard to raise another woman's kids. I got you in a real fucked up situation and I understand if you no longer want to be with me. I don't deserve a woman like you."

"Baby, I'm fucked up as well, so all is forgiven. I'm here because I want to be. Those kids need stability. In time, my heart will heal, but right now, we are a family. I will never turn my back on you or them. I'm not cut from that type of cloth.

"Why are you looking so sad?" Markese asked.

"I wasn't going to tell you, but I have to. Yesterday, I found out I was pregnant."

"Why you didn't want to tell me?"

"I don't want to get our hopes up. We both know what's going to happen. So, let's just prepare ourselves for the inevitable."

We both just sat there in silence for a moment. We knew this pregnancy wasn't going to be any different the others. Markese quickly changed the subject.

"How are the girls doing?"

"Aja is big as a house, ready to have that baby. She says that she's holding the baby in until you and Rahmeek come home. I think she's lost her damn mind. Nisa and Niyah being themselves, if you get my drift.

Markese smiled. "That's what's up."

"Look at you, still being head of the family worrying about all of us when we should be worrying about you."

"Don't worry about me. I'm Gucci. You just keep holding the family together."

"I will, baby."

We were informed that our visit was over so we said our goodbyes. I walked out of that jailhouse different from the way I walked in. at that moment, I knew my love for Markese could overcome anything. That nigga don't know it yet, but he better be ready to buy a bitch the biggest rock he can find when he get out. I deserve that much.

Chapter 32 - Markese

If it wasn't for my family, I would have been given up but I got to be strong. Seeing Trish made me realize how much I love her and how I can't live without her. Being locked up has given me all the time I need to reflect on the bad shit I've done. Things are going to be different when I get out.

If I get out.

Shit is not looking good for me or Rahmeek. Killa, Boogie, and Hassan had to leave town due to all the heat. They left without telling anyone where they were going, not even Nisa or Niyah. Those niggas got some shit up their sleeves. I know that Carmen is behind all this shit. I can feel it in my gut. If I ever get my hands on her, I'm going to torture that bitch to death.

Here comes this bitch ass CO Bradley. This nigga is always talking shit. I want to murk this nigga so bad.

"You have a visit, inmate."

"I don't want any visits. I refuse."

"You can't refuse a special visit."

"Do you know who it is?"

"Do I look like a fucking messenger? Get your ass up and get ready for the visit."

Bradley escorted me to an isolated visitation room and locked the door behind him. Now I'm sitting here nervous as hell. Special visits aren't anything but the State's Attorney with more charges. I heard the door unlock and Detective Jordan, the cop who initiated the raid and arrested us, walked into the room.

"Man, what the fuck you want now?"

"I'm here because you need me."

"What the fuck I need your ass for? You have done enough for me already," I said, standing up from the table.

"Just sit down and listen. Maybe your ass will be a free man next week instead of a fucking number for the rest of your life."

"I'm not a fucking snitch. You're wasting your time if that's what you're here for."

"Calm down. I'm not here for you to snitch. I'm here because of your mother."

"What the fuck you talkin about? You don't even know my mother. As matter of fact, I haven't even seen my mother."

"Markese, your mother and I go way back. I was with your mother back in the day. When I found out who you were, I tried to find her. I've been in contact with her since we arrested you. She asked me to see what I can do and I told her I couldn't do anything. I told her no because I knew you wouldn't approve of her dealing with me anyway."

"You damn right, but that's not telling me why you want to help."

"Because…" he paused like he had something serious on his mind. " I'm your father."

I burst out laughing. "Are you crazy? I don't have a father. I never have and I never will."

"I know you're shocked. But look at us. We're practically identical."

"Detective, you are killing me with this shit right now. I got enough on my plate. How can you help me out this jam?"

"I am the lead detective on this case. When I was interviewing Ms. Rodriquez at the hospital, she failed to let me know that you are the father of her children. She never told me about the history between her and Rahmeek either. My antennas went up instantly when I found out about this from Gail. Plus, I know where she is."

"And you're doing this because you think I'm your son?"

"I'm doing it because in my heart, I know that you and Aja are my kids."

"Man, I'm fucked up in the head, but I appreciate this."

"Keep this between you and me. Rahmeek has no idea about all of this. Return to your housing unit and act like this visit never happened. No one knows about this but us."

"Alright, I got you. On the real though, good looking out, Detective. Oh, yeah let me give you the number to some of my associates who may be able to help you out."

After dapping him up and getting escorted back to my cell, I didn't sleep at all. My mind was all over the place. After all these years, I finally have a reason to speak to my mother again. She definitely got some explaining to do. I'm not going to get my hopes up high because if anything can go wrong. I'm really fucked up about this nigga being my father. I can't imagine that my criminal ass got a pig for a father. It's official. I'm getting out the game.

Chapter 33-Trish

Game Over

Since I found out I was pregnant, I have been trying not to worry. I was glad Markese and I talked every day. I was surprised when Markese wanted me to meet up with a friend of his. He wanted me to meet him at a local diner. At first, I was skeptical when I realized it was Detective Jordan. As soon as I sat down, Detective Jordan handed me a piece of paper with an address on it. There were also directions to get to the address.

"What is this for, Detective?" I asked as I looked the paper over.

"That is the key to your husband's freedom. Carmen is being held at that address. You're the only one that can help right now. I have been trying to get in touch with his associates, but haven't had any luck. Time is running out so, you have to act quickly."

The detective got up from the table and left me sitting there. I immediately called Nisa and told her to meet me at my house. We were both pulling into my driveway at the same time.

"Trish, this better be good. I was in the middle of making my pick-ups."

"Come on in the house. I don't want to talk out here."

I handed Nisa the paper with the address on it.

"What is this?"

"That's where Carmen is being held at."

Nisa pulled her gun from her purse." Let's go get that bitch right now."

"Put that shit up, with your trigger happy ass! First, we have to get in touch with Killa, Hassan, and Boogie."

"They just made it back in town this morning. Let me call them right now."

Nisa called them and told them about the info we had. Killa, Boogie, and Hassan came over to my house and we went over the plans. The next night we would all go to the address. I couldn't believe I was about to set it off again. Markese needed me. I was more than happy to get that bitch.

The ride out to the location was not bad at all. When we arrived, there was a car was parked in front of the house. Detective Jordan had already informed us that, two agents were outside keeping watch. My nerves were all over the place. As I sat in the backseat, I prayed everything went smoothly. We parked the car about a block away from the actual location so that we would be unnoticed. We were dressed in all black. Killa, Hassan, and Boogie approached the police vehicle and fired several times. No gunshots were heard. They've been doing this a long time. They had the best silencers money can buy. Both agents were asleep they never seen it coming.

The door to where Carmen was at was unlocked. We all went inside. She was sleeping like a baby.

"Get the fuck up, bitch," I said as I smacked her across the face.

She instantly set up in bed. The look on her face was priceless. It was a look of fear and terror. We were all standing around her bed.

"Look, they made me tell on Rahmeek and Markese. I had no choice."

Boogie yanked her up from the bed. "Bitch, quit lying."

"Please, let me go. I promise I won't say anything." Carmen was begging and pleading.

"Shut the fuck up!" Nisa said, pistol-whipping her.

As Carmen lay on the floor crying, blood poured from her face. "Please, don't kill me," she pleaded. "My kids need me."

That was the ultimate insult. She did not care about them kids. I just started beating her ass. It took Killa and Boogie to get me off her ass.

"Grab that bitch. Let's ride," Hassan said.

Killa and Boogie grabbed Carmen and dragged her out of the house. Nisa poured gasoline all over the apartment and lit a match. She did the same thing to the police car with the two dead agents in it. I'm starting to think Nisa is a pyromaniac. She loves burning shit up.

Carmen fought and tussled the whole ride to her final resting place. Carmen begged and pleaded for her life, but it was too late. Once we made it to the cemetery, Carmen fought, screamed, and yelled, but it was useless. Killa, Boogie, and Hassan dragged her to a freshly dug grave. Nisa and I tied Carmen up and stuffed a rag inside of her mouth. She became tired and accepted her fate. We tossed her over into the grave inside of a coffin that was already occupied by a corpse. Her eyes got big as saucers when she realized she was being buried alive alongside her dead father.

We shut the coffin and began to cover it with dirt. The headstone was placed back in its place. No one would ever know what happened. I hoped that as Carmen was lying on top of her father she realized that all the bullshit was not worth it.

Carmen went to great lengths to ruin my relationship. In return, I'm taking her life. Carmen couldn't accept the fact that Markese no longer wanted her. She should have accepted that and moved on. I'm quite sure Carmen thought this is not supposed to be her ending. However, she sealed her own fate, when she fucked with this family.

She has now met that bitch named Karma that never takes a day off; not even holidays. At this point, she knew she had brought all this shit on herself. I pray that Carmen dies a slow and painful death alongside the very man who gave her life and in return, she took his. We sped out of the cemetery and rode back to the city. Our job was done. Hopefully, Markese and Rahmeek will be home soon.

Chapter 34 - Aja

I can't wait to have this baby. It seems like I been pregnant forever. I'm missing Rahmeek like crazy. I sleep in his t-shirts and boxers so I can have his scent on me when I sleep. I been visiting him every week, and I have been there for his court dates. It's getting harder and harder for me. I be crying and getting emotional. I can't take it anymore. Rahmeek doesn't want me to visit anymore since it's close to my due date. He doesn't want to take any chances.

I have been having pains like crazy, but King better stay in the oven until his daddy comes home. I know that's an unrealistic request because when it's time, it's time. I just want him to be present when his first son is born. I'm due next week. I'm praying for a miracle because that's exactly what we need. I just have to keep the faith and remain supportive for him and my brother. We ladies have to keep this family together and that's exactly what we have been doing. Since the night we killed Mont we have all become close. I was so happy when Nisa and Killa hooked up. They make the perfect couple. All she does is talk about him.

Trish, Nisa, and Niyah have been hanging out with me, watching over me since I'm about to pop any minute. Trish has been so stressed out and worried about the baby she is carrying. She had been spotting so Markese told her not to come to the hearing. Plus, she had a doctor appointment for an ultrasound to check on the baby's progress. When I went to visit him, he expressed his concerns for her health. I assured him she was doing fine. Although, Trish has been through a lot this year, she is stronger than all of us. Trish is the glue that is holding all of us together.

****

"Damn Aja, you're big as hell! that baby blew your ass up." Niyah said.

We were all sitting around the kitchen, smashing on all this food Trish cooked earlier.

"I know girl and Trish isn't helping. Look at all this food she cooked. She be in here feeding my ass."

"Your ass don't be complaining when you eating!" Trish laughed.

"I wonder what happened at the preliminary hearing today," Niyah said, changing the subject.

"Don't even mention it," I sighed. "I'm trying not to even think about it. Man, I will be so glad when I can give Rahmeek hug."

"I can't wait for you to hug me too," a male voice said from behind me.

I turned around and started screaming. I couldn't believe my eyes. Rahmeek was home…standing in our kitchen! Next thing I know Markese, Killa, Hassan, Boogie and some female I never seen before walked into the kitchen. There wasn't a dry eye in the house.

"Oh my God, Markese," Trish said while she and the kids were hugging him. "We missed you so much! How in the hell did y'all get out baby?"

"Judge threw out the charges," Markese smirked. "Lack of evidence. Let's just be thankful this shit is over."

"Hey, Boogie, aren't you going to introduce us to your friend?" I asked.

"Yeah, this is my girl, Stacy," Boogie said and introduced her to all of us.

As it turned out, Stacy was the one who helped Boogie, Killa, and Hassan when they went out of town. She and Boogie went way back. After reuniting, they decided to make it official. We welcomed her into our crazy family and told her to get ready because being a "hood wife" is bumpy ride.

Suddenly Rahmeek, Killa, Markese, Hassan, and Boogie all got down on one knees. One by one, they each asked us to marry them. Rahmeek asked me first.

"Aja, I never thought I would fall in love again. All that changed when I met you last year. You make life worth living. My life ain't shit if you're not in it. Would you please do me the honor of being my wife?" Rahmeek had tears streaming down his face and so did I.

"Yes, baby. I will be your wife." Rahmeek buried his head in my stomach and hugged me around my waist. Next, it was Markese's turn to ask Trish.

"Trish, I've been in love with you since we were teenagers. You were my first everything. I've slipped up over the years. Despite my fuck ups, you're still here. I took you for granted. I regret everything I put you through. I want to spend the rest of my life making you happy. Plus, I'm Clyde and I need my Bonnie. I won't last a day without you. Will you marry me Trish?"

"What do you think, Gabriella and Juan? Should I marry your Daddy?"

"Yes, yes, yes!" they both screamed and jumped up and down.

"Yes, I will marry you, Markese." Trish and Markese kissed and held each other tightly. At this point, everyone was crying. Next, it was Hassan's turn to propose to Niyah.

"I'm going to keep this short and simple. You have been my ride or die chick since we met. You stayed by my side when I had one foot in the grave. I love the fact that you are so loyal, and that's enough for me. Let's make this shit official. Will you marry me Niyah?"

"Hell yeah, I will marry you Hassan." Hassan picked Niyah up and spun her around.

Killa grabbed Nisa's hand and confessed his love for her.

"Right now, I'm taking a leap of faith. I have never been a one-woman man, but you have changed all that. When I'm with you, I'm grounded. You have a way about you that makes you stand out from other chicks. We have held each other down in these streets so I know you will hold me down as my wife. Will you marry me, Nisa?"

"Yes, I will marry you." Nisa bent down and kissed Killa on the lips.

Finally, Boogie proposed to Stacy.

"I know it's been years since we seen each other but, seeing you again brought back feelings. Being with you feels so right. After all these years, you still love a nigga. You hid us out when we were in trouble. In my line of work, that shit speaks volumes. I can't see me loving anyone else but you. Will you be my wife?"

"Of course, I will marry you.

At this point, we were all hugging and kissing one another and showing off our rings. This is the best day of my life. To think, a couple of months ago these niggas was at each other's head. God is definitely good.

"Everybody, I don't mean to break up this happy moment, but I have an announcement to make. My water just broke. It's time."

"Baby, what you mean your water broke? I don't think I'm ready."

"Rahmeek, me and this baby are ready. Now let's get out of here. I don't want to have my baby in the car."

Instantly, everybody was jumping up and panicking. I had to tell them to calm down so we could leave.

I was in labor for damn near ten hours. I was so happy when that painful shit was over. Our son King Rahmeek Jones was born, weighing in at nine pounds, twelve ounces. He's a big boy, just like his daddy. I'm not surprised because my baby put me through hell, but I would do it all over again for him.

Epilogue

It has been six months since the charges were dropped against us. Life couldn't be better. We are one big happy family. Ever since the day I saw my son being born, I have found a new sense of happiness. Besides Aja, I never knew someone could have my heart. Lil Rahmeek definitely has my heart in his pocket.

Aja and I have been doing great. She is a wonderful mother. Markese and Trish are hanging in there. She is seven months pregnant and the baby is healthy. Killa and Nisa are crazy as hell. They deserve each other. He really loves her. Niyah and Hassan are still going strong. Even Boogie and Stacy are still together, just as much in love as the rest of us.

After all that we have been through, we all took a much needed vacation to the Virgin Islands. Since we were in paradise, I got with the fellas and we all decided to marry the girls. They deserved it. Momma Gail and Mike joined us as well. Markese and Aja were glad their mother was clean. Thanks to Mike. They love the grandkids. Mike is good people. He definitely wants to be a part of her life.

Upon arriving to the Virgin Islands, we had already made arrangements for the wedding. We're so cool with our shit that we already ordered their dresses, shoes, and accessories. We also flew in Trish's whole staff from the Shop to do their hair and makeup. All the ladies have to do is show up.

I can't believe the whole crew about to tie the knot. We have been through some shit this year. We got some straight ride or die chicks. Man, they love us and remained loyal throughout everything.

THE WEDDING

"I can't believe we're all getting married at the same time on the same day. This is crazy," Niyah said looking in the mirror.

"I can't believe I'm getting married at all," Nisa shook her head. "Y'all bitches know I can't cook or clean. All I know how to do is put bullets in niggas. Killa better be lucky I love his ass."

"Oh no, bitch you love that dick .I heard y'all through the wall last night. He was giving your ass the business," Trish said.

"Hell yeah! that nigga be fucking my brains out."

"Aja, why are you looking so down? I thought you were ready for all of this?" Niyah asked.

"I am happy. I just have a funny feeling that something will go wrong. It always does. I'm ready to marry Rahmeek. My gut just don't feel right."

"Well take your ass to the bathroom and get your guts right. You about to kill my vibe on my wedding day. Ain't nobody got time for that," Niyah said.

"Before we do this, ladies, I just want to say thank you for accepting me on such a short notice. I see how close y'all are and how much you love those niggas. I really love Boogie and I want to spend the rest of my life with him," Stacy said through tears.

"Girl, it's cool. We're in this shit together. We're a family now. If Boogie loves you, we love you too," Trish said.

"Are you ladies ready? Your future husbands are waiting for you." the wedding coordinator informed them.

"Yeah, we ready let's do this shit" Niyah hollered.

Momma Gail and Mike wore all white and so did all the kids. Rahmeek, Markese, Killa, Hassan, and Boogie were standing beachside in white linen suits, waiting to receive their brides. One by one, each girl walked down the aisle to a song she picked.

Aja walked down the aisle to Share *My Life* by Kem.

Trish followed, walking to *Happily Ever After* by Case.

Then Niyah walked down the aisle to Tamia's *Spend My Life with You*.

After Niyah was Nisa. She chose *My Latest, My Greatest, Inspiration* by Teddy Pendergrass.

Stacy went last, walking to *Here and Now* by Luther Vandross.

After all the ladies met up with their future husbands, the Pastor prayed for their happy union. One by one, each couple confessed their love for one another and exchanged rings. As each couple stood held hands and looked into each other eyes, they knew everything they had been through was worth it because they had each other.

TO BE CONTINUED

Acknowledgements

First and foremost, I would like to thank my Lord and Savior who is ahead of my life. Without you nothing is possible.

To my wonderful parents Cornelia Hughes and Moses Williams Jr. Thank you so much for being the best parents in the world. Also, I would like to thank you for always believing in me.

To my beautiful sons Larry McCoy III and Latrell Moses McCoy everything I do is for you guys. I live and breathe for you.

To my siblings Micha, Tatiana, Sasha, Jason, Joseph, and Savannah I love you more than words could express. I love being your big sister.

To my Nieces and Nephews Shaniyah, Devontae Jr, Jamell Jr, Christian, and Ma'Kayla. Auntie loves you!!!

To my god children Angel, PJ, and Sa'Niirah God Mommy loves you so much!!!!

To my entire family both sides #OTF in my eyes. We all we got. It's too many of you to name, but you know who you are. LOL

To Talisa and Ramona, Thank you guys for always motivating me to follow my dream. I love you so much.

To my best friend, my ride or die chick Betty Green. It will forever and always be us against the world.

To all of my friends I love you ladies more than you will ever know.

Thanks, to all my readers for taking time out of your busy day to read my work. I really appreciate you.

A special thanks to, Myss Shan for, always responding to my text, emails, and inboxes. You believed in me when I was just a fan of yours with a dream.

Very special thanks to David Weaver, Myss Shan, and Jackie Chanel for taking a chance on me. I am forever grateful for this opportunity. I'm so glad to be a part of the TBRS and Black Starr Productions family.

I would like to dedicate this book to Chante McGhee who left this world way too soon.

If I forgot to mention anyone please blame it on my head and not my heart.

Contact Information

I hope everyone enjoys reading my debut novel. Please feel free to leave a review when you're finished reading it. Hit me on:

Facebook:http://facebook.com/patrice.williams.3975

E-mail: Mz.LadyP819@yahoo.com

Twitter: @MzladiiP_BSP

Instagram: MZLADYP819

Copyright Information

Living for Love and Dying for Loyalty

Copyright 2014 by Mz. Lady P
Published by Black Starr Productions
Cover Art by Brittani Williams
All rights reserved

This book is a work of fiction. Names, characters, places, and incidents either are the product of the author's imagination or are used fictitiously and are not to be construed as real. Any resemblance to actual persons, living or dead, business establishments, events, or locales or, is entirely coincidental.

No portion of this book may be used or reproduced in any manner whatsoever without writer permission except in the case of brief quotations embodied in critical articles and reviews.

Any inquiries can be made to:
blackstarr_productions@yahoo.com

Black Starr Productions Presents...

Formerly Titled Hustle Bunnies: A Rise to Power

By Shaunta'e

Cuz and The Hustle Bunnies have taken over the streets of East Hammond but come ups don't last forever. There are always those enemies known as greed, hate, and jealousy that live among us and can become a cancer within a team. Can Cuz, Precious, Toya, Shree, Neicey, and Sonya maintain their rise to power or will they succumb to these enemies and fall as a team?

Available on Amazon.com

CALLING ALL AUTHORS

Black Starr Productions is currently accepting submissions!

Black Starr Productions is currently accepting manuscripts. Send Submissions to Blackstarr_Productions@yahoo.com

Become affiliated with the one of the hottest teams in publishing.
#TBRS #BSP

If you have a finished manuscript that you would like to send for consideration, please send the following to blackstarr_productions@yahoo.com

Contact information

Synopsis

First 3 chapters in a Word DOC

If BSP has any interest in your work, the full novel will be requested.

Please allow 2-3 weeks for a response.

TABLE OF CONTENTS

Main Menu

Chapter 1 - Aja

Chapter 2 – Markese

Chapter 3 - Rahmeek

Chapter 4 - Aja

Chapter 5 - Trish

Chapter 6 - Markese

Chapter 7 - Rahmeek

Chapter 8 - Carmen

Chapter 9 - Aja

Chapter 10 - Trish

Chapter 11 - Aja

Chapter 12 – Markese

Chapter 13 - Trish

Chapter 14 - Carmen

Chapter 15 - Aja

Chapter 16 – Carmen

Chapter 17 - Trish

Chapter 18 - Markese

Chapter 19 - Rahmeek

Chapter 20 - Markese

Chapter 21 - Aja

Chapter 22 - Markese

Chapter 23 - Trish

Chapter 24 – Rahmeek

Chapter 25- Aja

Chapter 26 - Trish

Chapter 27 - Markese

Chapter 28 - Markese

Chapter 29- Carmen

Chapter 30 – Aja

Chapter 31 - Trish

Chapter 32 - Markese

Chapter 33-Trish

Chapter 34 - Aja

Epilogue

Acknowledgements

Contact Information

Copyright Information

Black Starr Productions Presents...

CALLING ALL AUTHORS

Made in United States
Orlando, FL
15 July 2025